A Waste of Good Paper

Sean Taylor

F

FRANCES LINCOLN
CHILDREN'S BOOKS

Friday the 6th of March

Pete says this is a writing book that he's only giving me and he says it's called JASON'S JOURNAL. And it's so I can write in it every day. And he said what did I think about that? So I said it sounded like A WASTE OF GOOD PAPER. And Pete says I can call it A WASTE OF GOOD PAPER if I want and I can write what I want. But SORRY PETE there's nothing I want to write.

Monday the 9th of March

I knew Pete was going to say I've got to keep writing in this book he got me because he reckons I'm good at writing. But that's not even actually true. I'm just ordinary at writing. But at least I can do it which is more than most of the dumb boys in this school can. I'm only good if you compare me to most of them because it takes them half a morning to write like TWO LINES.

Anyway Pete's getting on my nerves about it now and I haven't even got anything more to write except here's a joke.

A bear does a poo and out comes this great big STINKING PILE OF POO. Then along comes this rabbit and does a poo too. Except when the rabbit does the poo the poo comes out in these little round balls PLIP PLIP PLIP PLIP PLIP. And the bear's poo's this great big stinking pile. So the bear asks the rabbit, "How do you poo so neatly like that?"

And the rabbit says, "Oh it's easy for us rabbits. It just comes out in these little balls PLIP PLIP PLIP PLIP PLIP. What about you Bear? Look at all that stinky mess you do. I don't know how you ever clean your bum after making all that big mess."

And the bear says, "OH it's easy for us bears. We just pick up any rabbit that's going past and WIPE OUR BUM WITH THAT!"

Tuesday the 10th

I thought Pete would be sticking his nose in this book to see what I've done and be smiling away and telling me it's VERY GOOD like usual when we do writing work. But now he just told me it's PRIVATE so if I tell him DON'T LOOK AT IT then he won't. But if I want him to look at it then he's going to look at it.

And Pete will stick to that because he might be a smiley and jokey bloke most of the time but when he tells us he's going to do something he sticks to it like frigging SUPERGLUE. He's that kind of teacher. Which can be a pain in the bum.

But this time it's good news by me because I'm going to tell him DON'T LOOK AT IT. Then that means I don't even have to write ANYTHING now. Pete's clever at teaching and noticing things like when someone's going to punch someone in the head which happens all the time in our school. But you can trick him in other ways so easily it's a joke. Like now I can just sit here pretending that I'm WRITING WRITING WRITING WRITING WRITING WRITING WRITING WRITING and it's something really **THOUGHTFUL.** But actually it's just a load of crap and squiggles

and things that don't make sense BLAH BLAH BLAH BLAHDY BLUE BLUE BLUE BLUEDY BING BANG BANG BODDER BADDER B B B B B

Pete thinks I'm writing. Pete thinks I'm writing.

Pete thinks I'm writing something ALL ABOUT ME.

Pete thinks I've written two and a half frigging

pages about me. In fact I've written a pile of crap

nothing to do with me because WHAT'S

THE POINT of writing anything about me?

Wednesday 11th of March

I knew that would work yesterday. Pete looked as
happy as a dog with two tails because I was writing
away. But actually it was just like when he was
taking me to see about going to Halimer which
is a normal school unlike HERONFORD which is
where I am now and which is full of psychos with
BEHAVIOUR DIFFICULTIES who nobody wants in
a normal school. But maybe they're going to let
me into Halimer next year which is a bit amazing
and everyone says is GOOD NEWS.
So Pete went with me there to see it. And we got
the bus and then we were walking down this street
and Pete was chatting on about something he
thought I was going to be interested in which is
HOW YOU PLAY RUGBY. But I wasn't interested in
it and then we got to some road works and there's
a sign in the road on a stand with signs facing both

ways about the road works. And I ducked under it and hid there. And Pete keeps on walking and even talking as if I'm still there. And then he realises I'm not. And he looks round with a face like he's just swallowed a tin opener.

And he says, "Jason? JASON?"

BECAUSE HE CAN'T FIND WHERE I AM.

And he looks ahead to see if I've like run ahead. When how could I?

And he looks back to see if I've run back.

And he looks over the road and everywhere.

But I keep quiet.

And he walks back and he still can't see me.

And then I step out and say, "Just tying my shoelace Pete."

And he comes out with all this stuff about how I'll never get a place at Halimer if I don't stop mucking about. And we're late. And we've got

to get there on time because of the impression.
BLAH BLAH.
But the thing was you could see he actually
thought it was funny how I tricked him. And what
I was writing yesterday tricked him again because
today he never looked at it. He just made me sit
and

TRY

    TO

        WRITE

            SOME

                MORE.

So I asked him WHY AND WHAT'S
THE POINT?
And he says the point is because of the storyteller
and the drummer which is RICHARD AND
AARON. Richard is a DRUMMER. And Aaron
does STORIES and he does RIDDLES which

sometimes you can get and sometimes it takes ages to get.

They came here last year. Then they're coming again next week on Monday. And what it means is they come in every morning for two weeks.

And sometimes D Class which is our class does stories and writing work with Aaron and another class which is C Class does drumming and music with Richard.

Then we swap and my class does drumming and C Class is with Aaron for stories.

And after two weeks when it's the last Friday people come to the hall and we do a PERFORMANCE.

And the Heronford School GOVERNORS and PARENTS and some other people come to watch. Like last year THE LOCAL MP came but I didn't meet him. And the performance is our class and C Class playing the music we did and reading out poems and things we've written.

And last year I was meant to be in the performance and doing my drumming. It was A DRUM SOLO because I found out I was all right at drumming at least that's what Richard said. And everyone said my drum solo was going to be one of the best THINGS OF ALL in the performance and how it was HARD. But actually it was easy.

And my Mum was meant to come and be in the audience. But then the problem was that on the actual day what happened was I LOST IT.

So in fact when all the parents and people were coming in to go in the hall I was along the corridor trying to kick my teacher who was Lindsey who's left now. And Lindsey was trying to stop me and calling me by my whole name JASON DOOLEY which he always said when he was trying to stop me doing something.

And then along came Liam who acts all strict
like he's the TOP BANANA round here though
he isn't because he's the DEPUTY HEAD not the
actual HEAD. And he's always starting on me
because he hates me. And he tries to pretend he
doesn't hate me because he's a teacher. But I
don't try to pretend I don't hate him because WHY
SHOULD I? And there are people trying to go past
into the hall and Liam gets my arms and Lindsey
gets my legs so I can't move. But they can't stop
me shouting. And the people coming for the
performance are pretending not to look. But they
can hear.
And Liam's looking so UPTIGHT it looks like the
buttons on his trousers are about to burst. But he
tells me I'VE GOT A CHOICE which he always says
because he thinks it's good teaching rather than
just telling you what you've got to do.
"YOU'VE GOT A CHOICE," he says. And

Lindsey nods at that. "Carry on like this and you're out of the performance. But pull yourself together and you can join the others and do your drumming which everyone's looking forward to."

And I say back,

"YOU CAN STICK YOUR FRIGGING PERFORMANCE UP YOUR NOSE!"

And that was it. They pick me up and I'm struggling although I can't do much.

And I reckon that was when the local MP arrived because there was a man in his best suit like they wear on the telly. And he sort of blinks at Lindsey and Liam as they're getting me in the QUIET ROOM which is a room down the corridor where they put us to COOL DOWN. All that's in there is just a bench that's bolted to the wall so you can't throw it and a crap painting on the wall of some trees and a sun in the sky which is probably meant

13

to calm you down but actually WINDS YOU UP
because it's so crap.

Then next thing the door's being locked. And
Lindsey went off because he had to be with my
class for the performance and just Liam waited
outside.
But I did what I always do when I'm in the quiet
room which makes you wonder why they even
call it the QUIET ROOM because you can make
a LOAD OF NOISE if you SHOUT and do
KARATE KICKS on the door.
So I was JUMPING INTO THE DOOR and shouting
out that LIAM'S A PAEDOPHILE and all sorts of
other stuff he probably wasn't very chuffed to
hear seeing as everyone even in the hall could
probably hear it too.
And after a bit he unlocked the door and told me
in this whispery voice,

"STOP

and

TAKE A DEEP BREATH

and

CALM DOWN."

And he said we could go to the classroom till the
performance was over because it was a better
place to wait.

And I did STOP and TAKE A DEEP BREATH.

And I must have looked CALMED DOWN because
then Liam lets me out and holds up his hands to
show I've got to STAY calm. And he says there's
visitors and the performance is starting.

And it was true because you could hear everyone
was quiet in the hall now and the Head Teacher
who's WENDY was saying some sort of speech.

And Liam's standing there with his hands up so
I booted him bang between the legs.

And I think that's why he's hated me ever since.

And it's also why he comes to Heronford wearing
a thing cricket players wear to protect them
which is called a CRICKET BOX.
And he doubled right up and tried grabbing me at
the same time. But he didn't.
And I was out the FIRE EXIT to the playground.
And there's this fence all round it so you can't get
out or anything which is what I would do if
you could.
But I legged it round the back of the hall.
And Liam was charging after me. Then in through
the windows I saw my class sitting there with all
the drums and things.
And Richard the drummer guy is looking at them
with his eyes all wide because the performance is
going to start.
And there's this flower pot with something in it
growing that A Class planted. And I grab it and
swing it at a window to smash the glass in.

And Liam gets my arm to try to stop the pot.
But it's too late because it hits the window and
smashes like a black bomb of earth over the
window and me and Liam. But it didn't break the
window because the windows at Heronford are
special glass that won't break even if you hit them
with a table. Raju tried that last term and it only
broke the table a bit.

And I never even saw if the people in the hall
paid any attention. Because Liam got me on
the ground. Then the performance was carrying
on as if nothing ever happened. You could hear
drumming.

And Pete came out to help get me as well. And
there was a lot of trouble after that.

I lost my BONUSES and had to have these stern
lectures from Wendy which I tried not to listen to.

Then I had to sit and talk about it for ages with

Liam saying *EVER SINCE YOU WERE SMALL*
PEOPLE HAVE BEEN LETTING YOU DOWN
and going

on

   and

      on

         and

            on

               and

                  on

as if he knows everything there is to know.

And I had to write a letter to say sorry to Richard
and Aaron and to the charity that pays for them
to come.

And then my Educational Welfare Officer Marie
spends ages telling me all the same things as Liam.

And I had to pay for a new flower pot for A Class.

And Marie said I shouldn't have lost it like I did
even though I was having a hard time at home

with Mum and JON who was her boyfriend then.
But she said in fact things were getting so bad at
school and also at home that now I had a CARE
ORDER on me and I was going to live in a HOME.

And all that was what happened last year when
Richard and Aaron came. And it's why Pete's
saying he doesn't want anything like that to
happen again when Richard and Aaron come this
time. Because everyone or at least Pete and Marie
and Liam say it's been a good year for me this
year. And I'm back home living with Mum. And if
I can stop my aggressive behaviour and tantrums
and things this time with Richard and Aaron then
that's going to be a sign that I've left behind last
year and I can go to Halimer and everything.
And Pete's got this idea that I've got to write
in this book because he says if I get a habit of
writing about what happens every day then he

reckons it's the best thing to make it go better.
And everyone wants me to be in the performance
this year instead of what happened last year.
And Pete's an ALL RIGHT teacher. And he's miles
better than Lindsey because he knows how to stop
us fighting better. And when Lindsey left I didn't
care because he tried to be funny but he wasn't
and also he had a girl's name.
But even so it's a DUMB IDEA Pete's got about
this book. Because the problem last year was to do
with WHAT PEOPLE WERE SAYING ABOUT MY
MUM when she was meant to be coming to
the performance.
She didn't ever even show up. But people in my
class were dissing her all the time because I
said she was going to come to it. Like Raju and
especially BARRY HOLMES were saying she's
A WHACKO and she BELONGS IN THE FUNNY
FARM. And they're calling her OFF HER TROLLEY

and MRS DOOLALLY. And that was because the only time she came to something at Heronford she was laughing all the time when it wasn't even funny and then she fell asleep.

And Barry can talk because his mum looks like one of those whales that's stuck on a beach. And my mum isn't crazy. It's just because she was taking drugs all the time then. And it was them calling her MRS DOOLALLY that made me lose it and get put in the quiet room and kick Liam and throw the plant pot and everything.

And what happens if they start dissing her again like that this year? Writing anything in this frigging journal book isn't going to stop them doing that.

12th of March Thursday

I wasn't very smart because I left this book just
in my tray. Then I went for my supervision with
Liam. And that was all right compared to normal
because he didn't ask nosey questions about Mum
and if she's taking drugs again which is what
he always asks and which winds me up because
it's none of his business. And it was also all right
because Liam said it was a good week for me. And
that's true because I kept myself together and didn't
hit anyone.
Not even Raju.

But then when I got back to the classroom that
was the end of my GOOD WEEK.

In my class there's eight of us which includes me.
There's Nathan who I'm usually friends with. Then

Micah who's all right even if he supports WEST
HAM. Then Nazrul who's quiet most of the time
and he's the biggest in the class though nobody
much is scared of him. Then after that there's
Raju who's a little squirt who's always annoying
you because of what he's saying or because of
what he's not saying. Then there's Raymond who's
a nutter. Then there's Paolo who's even more of
a nutter and also he's like frigging SPIDERMAN
because last term he got on the roof of the school
and no one even knows how he got there. And
after that there's Barry Holmes who's UGLY AND
FAT and the best way to describe him would be
COMPLETELY CRAP AT EVERYTHING.
And when I got back from Liam everyone was
there except for Nathan who was away. Paolo and
Raju were on the computer. Micah and Nazrul
were with Pete by the board because they were
doing some maths about money. Then there's just

Barry Holmes and Raymond left. And they're in the quiet-reading corner on the quiet-reading beanbags.

And I come in and Pete tells me to do quiet reading like them.

So I look at the books. Barry's got the T-rex one because everyone gets that when Pete says DO QUIET READING. It's the biggest book by miles and it tells you all about a T-rex from when it comes out of an egg to when it became the dinosaur that can rip any dinosaur to bits.

But FATHEAD Barry's got that.

So I get a football book which is all right except I've read it about twice already. And Barry's got his big bum on one of the quiet-reading beanbags and Raymond's lying on the floor with his head on the other one. But I don't mind about that. I just get a chair and turn it round so I don't have to see Barry's ugly head.

And he looks like he's reading the T-rex book.
But when I'm sitting down I notice this little smile.
And I know that's because he's laughing at me.
And then I can see he's got this journal book Pete
gave me. And it's inside the T-rex book. And he's
reading it. And I didn't think about it twice. I slung
the chair right at him and smashed him right in
the head with it.

Then I say, "GIVE THAT!"

And Pete's shouting, "WHAT'S GOING ON?"

And I wish the chair properly knocked Barry out
like in a film. But he's not knocked out because
it's just a crap school chair. In fact he's laughing
and shuts the T-rex book tight so my journal's still
inside.

And he says, "THAT'S A CRAP JOKE ABOUT
THE RABBIT!"

And I know it's a crap joke because my mum's
ex-boyfriend Jon told me it. And all Jon's jokes

were the worst jokes you ever heard.

Then Pete's there with his hands on his hips like he MEANS BUSINESS.

But I try to punch Barry anyway because he's just lying there like a frigging slug on the quiet-reading beanbag.

And he swings the T-rex book just when I'm coming at him and it thumps into my lip.

And Pete gets me which he's good at because he's had training at it and also because he's a big bloke.

And he shouts, "STOP RIGHT NOW!"

And I say, "He's reading my journal book!"

And I want to kick Barry right in the face but I can't because Shabana who's the classroom assistant gets in between and she's trying to get the T-rex book off Barry.

Then it all goes quiet because Pete's holding me and Shabana's got the book. And although normally if you smash someone's head with a chair it means YOU'RE THE ONE IN TROUBLE

Pete doesn't get angry with me. He shouts at
Barry and tells him reading my journal book is
DISRESPECTFUL and it's PRIVATE and I've been
working hard writing it and not even him who's a
teacher is reading it.

And I'm thinking at least Barry can't have
read much because he's such a turkey brain HE
HARDLY KNOWS HOW TO READ.

And Pete is really frigging mad and Barry goes like
some dumb sheep which is what he is because he
might be a big fat boy but HE'S WEAK ON
THE INSIDE.

And Shabana's got my journal book out of the
T-rex book and she says Barry's got to STAND UP
and GIVE IT BACK to me himself and also say
HE'S SORRY.

And Barry does what she said sort of looking at
the ground and not with one of his USUAL CLEVER

SMILES on his face. And I get my journal book back. And Pete nods as if that makes it better now. But do you think that Barry Holmes saying sorry because he's GOT TO makes it better for me?

Pete and Shabana think it's over and Barry's still looking down. So I take the chance and punch him so frigging hard that this time he does drop like he's unconscious in a film.

He's got this ugly little short nose but I feel it go as if it's squashed right sideways on his cheek. And Barry's holding his hand on it and there's blood coming out and dripping on the quiet-reading beanbag and the carpet. Then Pete and Shabana bundle me into the corridor and Shabana dashes back in the classroom to see if Barry's ABOUT TO BLEED TO DEATH. And now it's me Pete's ranting at. And I can't even remember what he said. Something about Barry saying sorry and me having to RESPECT IT. But I couldn't care about that. I'm just glad I got Barry like I did. Except it means I go straight to see Liam and have to sit there like a lemon while he gets angry.

And then Wendy comes along and says Barry's got a BADLY INJURED NOSE and ARE THEY GOING TO LET ME INTO HALIMER IF THEY FIND OUT I DO THAT SORT OF THING TO MY CLASSMATES?

And she's going red. And I know from personal experience it's not a good sign when a Head Teacher starts going red. So I don't say anything back.

And she starts saying how I've got to LEARN TO MANAGE MY BEHAVIOUR and stuff I already know because I'm not completely stupid. Then when she finishes she pauses like she's waiting for me to say something. But I don't have anything to say.

And after a bit she gives up trying to get me to say anything and goes.

Then Shabana brings back Barry. And he's got this stupid bandage from the FIRST AID BOX on his nose that makes him look a complete fool.

And Liam gets me and him together and says we're being dumb because we're classmates and we don't mind each other if we're playing football in the same team. Which is true even though Barry Holmes plays football WORSE THAN A FRIGGING CARTHORSE. And he says if we try then we can get on all right.

Then he says we've both got to do something. Barry's got to SAY SORRY because of reading my journal book and tell me he WON'T DO IT AGAIN. Then I've got to say sorry for SMASHING HIS NOSE and also I'LL FORGET ABOUT WHAT HAPPENED AND LEAVE IT BEHIND.

So he starts with Barry. And Barry pulls a face like a baby who's dropped his dummy and says, **"I ALREADY SAID SORRY JUST**

NOW!"

And Liam tells him he can say it again.

So he says it but Liam makes him say it even
another time LOOKING PROPERLY AT MY EYES.

And he does. And he also says he won't read my
journal book any more.

Then it's my turn. And I'm just sitting there hating
Liam and Barry. And Liam says, "So what are you
going to say back Jason?"

And I say, "I know the rabbit joke's crap because
my mum's ex-boyfriend told it and all his jokes
were crap."

Then Liam gives me this UPTIGHT look and he says
to me it's not what I'm meant to say.

But I'm not saying anything else.

And he says I'm being STUBBORN and I've got to
say SORRY FOR HITTING BARRY and also I'm
going to FORGET WHAT HE DID.

BUT
I'M
NOT
SAYING
IT.

And Liam starts saying my whole life and the life of everyone in the school is going to get better if me and Barry can get on.

But I **SHAKE MY HEAD** because I don't want to forget what Barry did.

Then Liam says to me something like, "Think of this Jason. At this school you don't do everything you want to. But also you don't do everything you don't want to." Which is the sort of thing he always says. And it makes you wish you had a remote control that would mean you could just TURN LIAM OFF.

But then it's lunchtime anyway and Liam's not a

very happy man with me.

And Barry's even less happy because that bandage makes his face look like THE BACK-END OF A SAUSAGE DOG and he's got to go to his mainstream school after dinner which is the school that kicked him out. Because all of us got kicked out of the schools we were at before. And when you come to Heronford you're meant to go back to your MAINSTREAM SCHOOL some afternoons. And some boys like Nazrul and Micah go every afternoon. And some of the others just go on Thursdays.

And I'm the only one who doesn't go ever because my mainstream school is MOORCROFT which was the most crap place ever. And I was going back there one afternoon a week last term. But it DIDN'T WORK OUT. And I'd rather sit in a pigsty full of rubbish than sit in my classroom there.

So I'm the only one left when it's Thursday

afternoon. And that's all right in fact because
Pete gets quite chilled out and usually takes off
his trendy specs and rubs his face so that you can
see he's more relaxed than usual. And most often
he sets me some work that I can do quietly and
then he sits doing something on his laptop. Or
sometimes he lets me go on the computer to play
games with no little pain in the bum like Raju
looking over my shoulder saying it's his turn.
So I quite like Thursday afternoons.
Except this afternoon Pete's not happy with me
because of what happened with Barry. So when
I go in the classroom he picks up a pot of PLAY
DOUGH and says, "Why don't you play with this?"
And I say, "What's that mean?"
And he says, "It means it's time you grew up
Jason."
And he doesn't take off his trendy specs or let me
go on the computer or anything. He just goes on

about how considering how clever I am I don't half manage to do a lot of stupid things and all the usual stuff teachers say although it doesn't make anything better. And then he's saying Barry was wrong but then I was wrong as well and I've got to make things up with Barry and learn to get on with him. BLAH BLAH.

And I tell him I'm not doing it.

And Pete scratches this scar on his neck which if ever you ask him how he got it he says it was IN A FIGHT WITH A GRIZZLY BEAR.

Then he says the next best thing is if I write down about what happened in my journal book.

And that's this that I've done.

And he also tells me not to leave my book lying around where just anyone can find it. So I've got to take it home or leave it in his desk drawer.

Then he told me to think carefully about what to say to Barry in the morning. And I already

know what to say is HE'S AS DUMB AS A
WOODEN CHICKEN and his mum looks like
THE LOCH NESS MONSTER and if he touches
my book again I'LL MAKE HIM WISH HE WAS
DEAD.

Friday the 13th of March

Today it's FRIDAY THE THIRTEENTH and
everyone was saying that meant it was going to be
bad. AND IT WAS.

On the minibus it already started badly because
I thought Barry Holmes wasn't going to show
up because his nose was so injured. But the
minibus went to his place like usual and he gets
on and there isn't even anything much wrong
with his nose. He told Keith the driver it was only
SPRAINED.
And who the hell ever heard of having a
SPRAINED NOSE?
Then we get to Nazrul's house and he hasn't even
woken up. Nazrul must have a potato for a brain
to be that much of a BUTTHEAD if you ask me.
Anyway we have to wait in the minibus and Barry

Holmes is going on about how his dad got in an argument with the man in the corner shop because he wouldn't put out his fag. Then when the man in the shop made him get out his dad took down his trousers and PRESSED HIS BUM ON THE WINDOW. And you could see Barry thought that was the funniest thing that ever happened in the history of the world. And he was saying he'd do it too. And I was sitting there and the thought of BARRY'S DAD'S BUM or BARRY'S BUM pressing against a window was spoiling my appetite for breakfast. Because Barry's face is enough to put you off eating NEVER MIND HIS BUM.

And Nazrul still didn't come out because his mum was probably telling him to eat his HAPPY FACE PANCAKES or something. Then he finally arrived still doing up his trousers. And we get to school and I hoped Pete might just forget it from yesterday but

NO
SUCH
LUCK

because he's got this LISTEN CAREFULLY
LOOK. And as soon as I get there he starts on
again about how I've got to learn to MAKE AN
APOLOGY and not try to GET MY OWN BACK
ON BARRY.

And I say back I don't care.

And Pete's trying to be his usual smiley self. But his
trendy specs are flashing because he wants to get
me to do what he wants. Then he says if I won't
SAY SORRY AND LEAVE IT BEHIND then he's
not having me in his class together with Barry.
But I'm not doing it whatever he says. And I tell
him. And he says that means I've got to go and be
in B Class till I change my mind.

So next thing I'm spending the morning with these kids I don't like much who still think getting REWARD STICKERS is a cool thing. And the teacher is Danielle. And they've got this topic which is BEAN SPROUTS. So they've all got a frigging bean sprout which has sprouted when they planted it on a bit of wet paper. And they know all about what the names of the parts of the bean sprout are.

And there's a little kid called Matthew who's showing me his bean sprout like it's the FA Cup or something when it's just a frigging bean sprout. Then the activity is they've all got to draw their bean sprout in their science books. And I haven't even got a science book or a bean sprout. So I have to do it on a bit of paper. And I have to share a bean sprout. And Danielle asks who's going to share their bean sprout. And this boy McShane says that's all right so I can draw his.

Then we start and I try it but I'm not very good at drawing. And it doesn't look like McShane's much good either. So I joke with him that his picture looks MORE LIKE A DUCK THAN A BEAN SPROUT. And he doesn't seem to like that. It's just a joke but McShane doesn't get the point because he starts dissing me under his breath. Then he changes his mind about sharing his bean sprout. And Danielle doesn't notice because she's helping Matthew. But McShane moves his bean sprout so I can't see it now.

And he says, "Draw your own."

And how can I because the whole point is I don't have a bean sprout?

Then McShane's got his back to me and I don't really care about it because I don't even want to draw a frigging bean sprout in the first place. But it gets worse because this boy Lewis is flicking a ruler and it knocks McShane's bean sprout so it goes on the floor. And McShane straightaway tries to knock Lewis's bean sprout on the floor as well. Except Lewis gets it out the way. Then the two of them are shouting about bean sprouts. And Lewis is saying it was an accident and protecting his bean sprout with his ruler because McShane looks like he's going to SQUASH IT FLAT.

And McShane's yelling out, "YOUR BEAN SPROUT'S DEAD MAN!"

And God knows what was going to happen. But then Josh who's their classroom assistant came and picked up McShane's bean sprout and showed him it was all right.

And I just looked at these giant butterflies that C Class have made that are hanging off the lights. And I'm thinking I'm going to be pleased when it's the end of Friday the thirteenth because being with these crazy kids almost makes me miss Barry Holmes.

But at least when I ask Danielle if I can just write in my journal book instead of doing bean sprouts she says all right. So that's what this is I'm writing.

Then it was time for dinner so we had dinner and I had to sit and eat it with B Class. And everyone in my class was falling about laughing because they thought that was SO FUNNY.

And I've got to sit next to Danielle and I was sick of being in B Class by then. And Danielle is a vegetarian which I think is a pretty weird thing to be because I've hardly eaten a vegetable in years. And it means you can't eat burgers unless they're BEAN BURGERS. And so instead of fish and chips which was what we had she had this other thing with chips that she said was SOYA. Whatever it was it looked a weird colour and I wouldn't touch it with a barge pole. And I'm sitting there just trying to eat my dinner. But she starts talking on

about her soya thing and says I should have one
because it would be good for my health. And I say
back, "It might be good for my health but I want
something that's good for ME."

And at least that makes her laugh.

Then Pete's coming across and he wants to know if
I've changed my mind and says it's the last chance
because Barry's going to his MAINSTREAM and I
won't see him till Monday.

And I'm thinking I don't want to spend all afternoon
with B Class any more. And also it's better having
Pete as a friend rather than an enemy.

So I say to him, "Yeah."

And Pete says, "You'll say sorry to Barry and also
forget about what he did?"

And I nodded.

Then Pete says, "FAB AND GROOVY."

And he says thanks for putting up with me to
Danielle and takes me across to our table.

Then I say what I have to say to Barry. Although I don't mean it. And Pete tells us to shake hands. And we do it.

Then I sit back at my class's table and Pete starts saying this speech about how me and Barry are good examples because we're leaving behind what happened. But nobody's actually listening because they're more interested in their fish and chips. And Pete's looking chuffed anyway. And he starts tucking back into his food. And at least I'm feeling better to be back with my usual class.

Then Barry goes off taking his SPRAINED NOSE with him. And the others who are going to mainstream go. And it leaves just me, Raju, Paolo and Raymond there in the afternoon.

But it's Friday the thirteenth so that means something else is probably still going to go wrong. And it does.

Everything was all right at first because Pete
was happy with me and everyone seemed in a
good mood now. And he let Raymond go on
the computer. Then he was going to do literacy
worksheets with Raju which meant me and Paolo
could do quiet reading. And that's all right by me.
I get this new book which is a book of funny poems
mainly about monsters. And Paolo's got a book as
well. But Paolo hardly knows how to read. So like
normal he wants to chat instead. And what he
says is he thinks Raymond is MAYBE A ROBOT.
And I don't know why but that CRACKS ME UP.
And I wasn't even going to listen to Paolo. But
I'm laughing because I think he's PROBABLY
RIGHT ABOUT RAYMOND.
And Pete says get on with our reading quietly.
And Raju pulls a face like he knows what we were
laughing about when he doesn't.
And Raymond's staring at his game like a robot.

Except he's got asthma and you'd have to be pretty dumb to make a robot with asthma. And I say that to Paolo and he starts laughing so Raymond looks round behind his glasses and he tells us to SHUT UP. But it's too late now and I can't stop laughing. Then there's the music that means Raymond's lost the game and he pushes back his chair. But he does it so it leans backwards. And my leg's stretched out so the chair leg catches on my foot. And next thing Raymond falls over backwards and whacks his head on the quiet-reading shelves.

It was like a clown falling over. And he didn't hit it so badly. And Paolo and me are laughing. And Pete jumps up to help Raymond get up. And he's smiling a bit too. But Raymond gets up and he thinks I did it and I KICKED his chair over and he just flies at me.

And the thing is that most of the time Raymond

is sort of slow and quiet and just blinks into his glasses which is why he's like a robot. But when he loses it then he can REALLY LOSE IT and not even Pete can stop him. Pete can handle any of the rest of us. But sometimes it needs three teachers to hold Raymond down. Because when Raymond loses it he doesn't fight in a normal way. It's more like he suddenly becomes an octopus with loads of arms or something. He goes

COMPLETELY NUTBAG.

And his elbows are flying around and he throws everything about. And this time it's quiet-reading books and also the sheets with our reading targets going everywhere and mainly aimed at me. And Pete tries to stop him doing it. But he can't completely and he says to Raju, "GET LIAM! TELL HIM IT'S RAYMOND!"

Then meanwhile Raymond's trying to pick up the classroom printer to throw it at me. And Pete's saying things to stop him but it's like what he says just bounces back off Raymond's ears. And I'm trying to get out the way. Then it's Wendy Raju brings in. And she and Pete manage to get Raymond still. And they try calming him down by asking WHAT HAPPENED. And he's shouting out things and breathing like he needs his asthma thing and calling me names and calling my Mum names and saying I kicked over his chair. And I say straightaway I DIDN'T. But Wendy never saw what happened and Pete didn't either. So they're not sure if I did it.

And Wendy's saying it'd better not be me because I was in enough trouble for one day.

And I say to them, "I never touched his chair!"

But Raymond says I did.

And Wendy asks Paolo. But Paolo doesn't know because PAOLO'S AS MAD AS A BOX OF FROGS.

But then Raju tells her he saw.

He says IT WAS ME because he saw me kick

Raymond's chair.

And that was it.

That really MADE MY DAY.

I look at Raju and say, "HOW CAN YOU EVEN

KNOW? YOU WERE DOING WORKSHEETS!"

But Raju said HE SAW IT.

So what made me explode wasn't even Raymond

throwing half the classroom at me. It was all

because SNOTHEAD RAJU said A BUNCH OF

LIES to get me in trouble.

And next thing it's me shouting at RAJU and

saying IF HE OPENS HIS MOUTH AGAIN I'LL

BREAK HIS JAW.

And although I never even went near him or

touched him or anything Pete got hold of me and

he said STOP OTHERWISE I WAS GOING IN THE

QUIET ROOM.

And Raju's looking back with this sneaky look that's even worse than when Barry Holmes is smiling.

And Wendy tells me to stop and she says DO I WANT TO BE IN TROUBLE? And tells me I HAVEN'T BEHAVED SO BADLY SINCE THIS TIME LAST YEAR. And also IS THIS HOW I'M GOING TO BE BEHAVING ON MONDAY WHEN RICHARD AND AARON COME?

But I didn't stop. So next thing I'm in the quiet room. And Pete's looking through the door as if he wants to send me on a journey that's one-way to AUSTRALIA.

And he won't let me out even though I said I didn't do it.

And the one good thing is I said if I was going to be in there then at least could I have my journal book to write in. And he gives it to me. So that's this I'm writing now.

Saturday 14th of March

It's Saturday so I'm not at school or anything. But I'm writing this because of what's happened. And that is my mum's ex-boyfriend JON SHOWED UP.

I don't know where he'd been. Mum said maybe he was locked up because I know she went to the police about him. But it was already night time and the doorbell went and I opened the door. And there he was looking pretty much nothing like when I saw him last. And he smiled and everything at me but even so he looked in a right state. He was older and thin which he never used to be because he had big muscles because he was in the army for a bit. And he needed a shave.
And also BOTH HIS ARMS WERE BROKEN.
It wasn't the whole of his arms. One of them had plaster round the wrist and the other had plaster

round the wrist and hand.

But his eyes were just the same little blue eyes
shifting round. That was the same as before.

Mum was watching TV and she said, "Who is it?"

So I told her, "It's Jon."

She turned off the TV straightaway. Then she
came to see. And I didn't stay around. I could see
on Mum's face she wanted him to just shove off
at first. And I thought they were going to start
shouting at each other or something because Mum
told me she wasn't letting Jon in ever again.

But in fact they talked quietly and I could hear
Mum asking things.

Then Jon was saying, "Please. Just this once. Just
this once."

And I didn't want her to let him in or anything
because of what Jon did when he used to come
here.

Him and Mum went out together for ages. So in

fact when I was little he pretty much lived here. And it was all right at first because me and him watched football together. And he liked playing penalty shoot-outs in the park. And also he taught me how to bend the ball when you shoot. And Mum got him to get me my bike on my birthday which is a kind of BMX with proper BMX tyres and a BMX saddle. And I've still got it. And in fact I even liked having him as a sort of step-dad.

But then when he was around before was when Mum started taking drugs all the time. He got her into that.

And then Mum started taking drugs so much she couldn't stop it. And she got all thin. And first of all she told me it was a sort of medicine she needed. So I thought she was ill. But then you could tell it wasn't medicine. It was just drugs.

And that was when her and Jon had fights that nearly made your head explode. And Jon twice gave Mum a black eye. And when he hits you it's not like Barry Holmes hitting you. It's hard like metal because he's been locked up for violent offences before.

But Mum let him keep on coming back because he was the one bringing her drugs. And sometimes he used to give them and sometimes she paid him. I know because every time Jon showed up a bit later Mum went in her room and came out and you could tell just from how she looked that she'd taken drugs. And it was like she wasn't really there. And if Jon didn't come round then she didn't have any drugs. And then she acted like she had ANTS IN HER PANTS non-stop and shouted at me about any little thing.

And I know what she took is called SMACK and HEROIN because at school Liam came and talked about different drugs. And he says it makes you in a good mood. But her and Jon never seemed in A GOOD MOOD. And Jon whacked me and kicked me lots of times though never when Mum could see. And the worst thing was something that I never told anyone about. Because after he did it he said I've got to keep quiet about it or he'll make me and Mum both wish we were dead. And from the way he looked when he said that you know it's true.

And I saw him punch Mum so hard she fell right over the sofa even though he thought I didn't see that. Then another time he went mad and he didn't even care that I was seeing what he did. And he pulled Mum's hair and hit her head on the cupboard in her bedroom. And those were some of the things that Jon did. And in the end she did give him the push for good and said she wasn't ever letting him back in the flat. And he never gave her the keys back so she had the locks changed so he couldn't get in. But then the only way she got rid of him completely was by going to the police.

Anyway Mum let Jon in. And he comes in the living room. And he stands there and he's all smiling and everything as if he couldn't even remember all the times he battered Mum and me. Then next thing he sits on the sofa right where I sit and sits there looking at the TV like he owns the place. And he lights a fag. And he's calling me JACEY and trying to be friendly to me but really he just talks to Mum. And she's putting the kettle on. And when she's in the kitchen he calls out to her that what he really wants is a wash so can he use the bathroom? And she says of course and gets him a towel and he doesn't even wait for the tea she's made him but goes in the bathroom.

And as soon as it was just me and Mum I say to
her, "Why did you have to let him in?"
And she says, "You know me and Jon go back a
long way. And he's stuck isn't he? He can't even
use his hands."
And I said, "What happened?"
And she said, "He broke his wrists and also a
thumb or something. He was doing this decorating
job and leaning out a window he was painting.
Then he fell out."
You could hear Jon was filling the bath.
And I say, "You've got to be bit of a prat to fall
out a window you're painting haven't you?"
And Mum starts laughing but then she says, "Sshh."
And then I say, "Anyway why's he got to come
round here even if he fell out a window?"
And Mum says, "He can't work so he doesn't have
money even to pay his rent. And he can't go back
there till he's got it."

But I still didn't know why that meant she had to let him in.

And she says, "He told me he's really sorry about all those things that happened before. But he's got his act together. And he did rehab like me. So he's off the drugs now. And he says he feels better for it like I do. And it's just tonight he needs to stay."

Then I say, "HE'S SLEEPING HERE?"

And she says, "There's no one apart from me who can help him."

And it's too late now because he's already here and in the bath. So I don't say much more.

Then Jon was in there for an hour or something. And when he came out he was shaved and looking a bit more like he did. And I was sitting in the kitchen.

And Mum was in there getting my clothes for school washed. She asks what he was doing in there so long and Jon says RELAXING. And Mum sets the washing machine going.

Then Jon sits on the sofa. And seeing as he couldn't use his hands he was pretty nifty with the remote control to put on Sky Sports News. Then Mum made some food which was chicken dippers. And you could see Jon was hungry.

And after it he was the one who did the washing up even though he could only do it slowly because his arms were broken. And he never used to do that when he was here before. And at least I didn't have to do it FOR ONCE. And Mum said to him he seemed a lot different. Then Jon asked what he was like before.

So Mum said straight off, "A GORILLA."

Then Jon started pretending to be a gorilla when he was washing up. So then we were all laughing a bit. Then Mum said it was time for me to go to bed and she was tired so she was going to bed too.

And I didn't mind like I usually would on Saturday because with Jon there I didn't even feel like staying up. And he says he's going to crash out too and he said THANK YOU because he was feeling a lot better.

Then Mum got him some covers so he could sleep on the sofa and at least that was better than before because he used to always sleep in Mum's room. And that was where they always had arguments.

And I'm in my room now writing about it. And I don't know what it's going to be like if Jon starts coming round like he used to. Because when they were still going out together Mum always used to say Jon wouldn't be coming back again but he just kept coming round and coming round. And she kept taking drugs. And all I can remember from then was them having flaming rows. And Jon saying they'd be having a better time if I wasn't around. And Mum being sick down the toilet.

It was the worst time I can remember because all that happened at school was I got in trouble. And Mum got the sack from her job at ASDA. And everything went so wrong they put a CARE ORDER ON ME. And I ended up having to go and live in a HOME. And I went and it was the worst dump you've ever seen. You got locked in. And I don't like even thinking about it.

And I'm not even writing anything about when I was in there because I hated it so much.

Sunday

I didn't get up till late. I woke up a few times but
then I thought about Jon being back here. So I
just lay there and kept going back to sleep. But
then there was a smell of cooking breakfast and I
remembered that from when Jon was here before.
He always said it was called JON'S FAMOUS
SUNDAY FRY-UP. He did training to be a chef
so he knows how to cook. And it was bacon,
sausages, beans, tea, toast and everything.
So I got up at last and Jon and Mum were sitting
there together in the kitchen. And Jon looks at
me and shouts out, "HAPPY CHRISTMAS!"
And there was his whole breakfast on the table.
He'd even been and bought the tomatoes from
up the road.
So Mum tells me to come and have something.
And Jon's got these photos on his phone of a

63

holiday he went on in Jamaica. He starts telling me about it and showing us him at this hotel with its own beach. And when you go there you can get everything for free you want. Like beer or pizza, popcorn or burgers or anything if you want. And I ate loads of the breakfast and Jon was saying a lot of things about his friends and holidays and how good life was for him now because his life is different.

And he asked what new things Mum does. And she said she didn't get out much and not much had changed because we were in the same old flat and I'm the same old Jason and all that's really different is she's got the job in the shoe shop which is all right.

And they didn't say much to me. And I was mainly just eating when they were talking. Except Mum asked if I liked the breakfast. And I nodded and she said even the toast tasted better than if she made it which was true. Then I just let them carry on talking because there was a game starting on the telly.

Then I was watching the game for a bit. And Jon comes smiling in and lights a fag and watches it too which was all right because we both know about football and it's better watching with someone else. But it was a crap game. And Jon sits complaining most of the time and says it would be more interesting watching TWO SNAILS CLIMB UP A WALL. But we still watched to the end though. And Mum was ironing my clothes for school. And after the game they showed how the camera filmed this fan who went to sleep during the second half and then suddenly woke up when there was a goal. And Jon was laughing about it and so was I. And Mum comes in to see it and she says we two aren't much better ourselves cos we're sitting on the sofa staring at the TV like we're half dead.

And I carry on watching the telly but I say I'm going to take my bike down to the ramp by the river. They say it's an ADVENTURE PLAYGROUND they built down there but it's not really. There was a ZIP WIRE but someone nicked the wire off it so that was the end of that. And it's got one ramp that's not very big and a pipe thing that's meant for skateboards. But nobody much goes there on skateboards. Mostly it's some of us who've got bikes who go there. We try tricks like you see on the telly. But we can't do them properly because none of us has got a proper BMX except for one boy called Ollie. And he can't do much on it. So in fact what you see most is us FALLING OFF AND CRASHING. And there's usually a few of us down there on Sunday. And there wasn't much sign of Jon getting up off the sofa. So I felt like going there.

But then when I say it Jon looks at me and goes,

"Jacey. If you're going out you can do me a favour."

And that was like he used to say when I was small. It was how he always used to say it. YOU CAN DO ME A FAVOUR. Then he'd say he needed me to take something somewhere or pick something up somewhere.

And always he said it was secret so I couldn't tell Mum. And back then I had a thing that I was going to be in the army. And Jon used to say it was training for that because he said when you're in the army you have to learn to go on missions and get back safely without getting stopped.

So every time I took something for him he used to say, "Off you go soldier!"

And I sometimes made up in my head that I was taking a secret message that was going to save people from being in a war.

And I didn't even mind about it at first because
it was something to do. And also I was collecting
football stickers and Jon bought me stickers for
my album when I did things for him. So I was
always giving an envelope to someone outside the
pub or by the toilet in the park then taking the
money they gave me back to Jon.

And he said if the police ever asked me about
what was in the envelope I had to just say I
FOUND IT IN THE STREET. And I didn't know
what I was taking at the start. But the people
nearly all looked like Mum did when she took
drugs. And you could tell what made them get
like that was taking drugs. So after a bit I knew
that Jon was getting me to sell drugs for him. And
it was because he wouldn't get in trouble for it
because nobody thinks a kid's going to be
selling drugs.

Then one time he got me to give this envelope to

a man who was down by the river where the ramp is now. And he was meant to pay twenty quid. But the man took it and said, "I already paid," and then walked off.

And I said to him, "Jon said it's twenty quid!" But the man didn't even look back.

So I went and told Jon. And straightaway he whacked me right in the head which was the first time he ever hit me. And he got really mad with me because of that. And he grabbed my neck and said, "What are you? Thick?" Then he shoved me on the sofa and he says, "Sit and watch children's TV! You're a waste of effing space like your mother!"

And after that I didn't like doing things for him any more. But I had to because if ever I said NO to him then he started hitting me or saying he was going to.

And I think Jon could tell I was remembering all that because he smiles away like I was meant to forget all that. And then he says, "Jacey. I'd go myself but it's not good for me. The doctor said I need to rest so I can get back to work. But you could nip over on your bike couldn't you?"

And I just carry on watching the telly.

Then he says, "It's my mate GIRAFFE. He borrowed some paint brushes and I need someone to pick them up because I need them."

And I say, "GIRAFFE?"

And Jon nods and says, "It's what people call him. It's because he's from Africa somewhere. And he's tall."

I say, "Yeah?"

And Jon nods and says, "And the paint brushes are expensive SABLE ONES. Giraffe borrowed them because he's doing up his house. But he called me to say he's done with them. And I'm going to need them for when I go back to work."

Then Mum says, "You can help Jon out can't you

Jason?" And she asks him, "Where is it your friend

is?"

And that's because she doesn't know about what

used to happen before.

"Tavistock Street," says Jon. "Giraffe's house.

Number 25. It's one of the new houses up the end

of Tavistock Street."

And Mum says, "Go on Jason. Give Jon a hand. He's

been in the wars."

And Jon says, "See if you can get the brushes for

me Jacey. Then I'll be heading off."

And I liked the sound of that. And I did want to

get out the flat anyway. So I got my bike and

I did it.

The sun was shining through the clouds outside.

But it was still cold so you could see your breath in

the air. I go past the building site that's normally

noisy but it's quiet because it's Sunday. After it the main road goes away from the river and Tavistock Street is up there. I know because it's almost the way you go to get to Heronford.

Then I get to the house Jon said and I ring the bell. And after a bit the door opens but on one of those chains you get. And a man looks out and you don't need to ask if he's Giraffe because he's this bloke who looks like a basketball player because he's about EIGHT FEET TALL.

And I say to him, "Jon wants me to get his paint brushes for him".

And then the door just shuts. And I don't know if I'm meant to wait or what because he didn't even say anything. But after a bit the door opens with the chain still on. And the man passes out this packet in a shopping bag with tape round it. And he says, "Tell Jon his paintbrushes are pure pleasure!"

And he's looking out at me as if that's really
FUNNY what he's just said or he thinks I look
FUNNY or something. Then he rubs his tongue
round his teeth and stands there looking. But I
don't say anything. I just ride off without saying
anything.

And I didn't even go to the ramp. I just went back.
And Mum and Jon were sitting in the kitchen
drinking tea. And Mum's writing a shopping list for
the supermarket. And I give the packet to Jon.
And he squeezes it and says to me, "Good man
Jacey!"

And he drinks his tea and smiles. Then next thing
he's saying THANK YOU to Mum. Then he just
goes.

And when Mum gets back from shutting the door
I think she's going to look like she always did when
Jon left which was this face like SOMETHING

BAD WAS OVER. But she doesn't. She doesn't really have any look. She just sits down and is writing the things on her list.

Then she says to me am I going with her over to ASDA?

But I said, "I just got in."

So she said she was going on her own. And she said I was never much help anyway because she was remembering when we got the taxi back from ASDA before Christmas and I forgot a bag of shopping on top of the taxi. Then when the driver started it fell off and a VAN RAN OVER IT.

And I was laughing a bit about that. But also I was thinking about Jon. Because I don't want him back here another time. Because when he's not here then you can just forget about all the things that happened. And Mum says our flat is like living in a BATHROOM CABINET and it's SMALL ENOUGH without having Jon prowling round.

And I asked Mum. I said, "What's going to happen with Jon now?"

And she looks at me as if she doesn't know.

And she says, "Jon's got to sort things out for himself." And, "I don't reckon he'll be back."

Then she went over to ASDA. And I'm just here writing this.

Monday 16th of March

I wasn't very thrilled it was ANOTHER MONDAY
because it was frigging freezing and I could hardly
wake up. So I lay there thinking that if SNEAKY
BLABBERMOUTH RAJU tries anything again I'm
going to shove his head down the toilet and flush
it. Then in fact just the thought of spending a
whole day with Raju and Barry and Liam stressing
me out at school put me off getting out of bed
ever again.

When I felt like that at my old school I just stayed
off with pretend flu or something. And Mum didn't
mind. But now I'm at Heronford she hardly even
lets me miss school when I'VE GOT REAL FLU.
So she made sure I got ready for getting the
minibus. Then when we got there I saw Richard
the drummer and Aaron the storyteller were
there which I'd forgotten about. So that meant

it was going to be a change at least. Then the morning started normally. We get breakfast which is toast with NUTELLA or MARMITE or JUST BUTTER.

And then SQUASH or TEA which I usually have because Shabana makes a good cup of tea.

And Pete's chatting away and being cheerful like always at breakfast. And he says we've all got to say WHAT ARE OUR TOP THREE ENGLAND FOOTBALLERS OF ALL TIME. Then after we've been chatting on about that he says we've all got to say OUR TOP THREE MONGOLIAN FOOTBALLERS of all time? And that's just Pete being a FUNNY MAN.

But even so Barry Holmes comes up with someone he says is a Mongolian player who plays for BLACKBURN ROVERS. And everyone's laughing because you know that's just Barry Holmes being a WISE GUY like usual. And even Barry knows that because you can tell from his stupid smile on his face. And the way his eyes go shifting around when he's smiling makes me think about how Jon was sitting there at our place all weekend smiling away.

Anyway then Pete's got this thing he's started this term. We have to do it every morning and they don't do it in any class except ours. And if you ask me it's A WASTE OF TIME but Pete obviously thinks it's a BRILLIANT IDEA of his. He's got this chart on the wall with our names and bits of paper that have got FEELINGS on. And we sit on the comfortable chairs. Then each of us has to tell everyone what feeling we're feeling. So it's things like HAPPY and SAD

and a load of others. And then we have to stick the feeling that we say next to our name.

And what I always do is get the one that says ALL RIGHT.

And Pete's not especially chuffed about that
because his whole idea is we're meant to SAY OUR
REAL FEELINGS. But every time I just choose
ALL RIGHT anyway.
And sometimes Pete says to me, "Are you SURE
you're feeling ALL RIGHT Jason?"
So I tell him, "Yeah."
And Pete nods because he tries to be very
FRIENDLY when we're doing feelings. But
underneath you can feel he's just DYING for me
to say I'm feeling AGGRESSIVE or CONFUSED or
something like that.
But that's his tough luck because all I'm saying
is I'm ALL RIGHT.

Anyway once we'd got our feelings done then
Aaron the storyteller man shows up and we're with
him. And Liam comes in and sits in with us too.
So that's a sign they don't want more trouble with

Richard and Aaron this year. Because I DON'T
think Liam was there because he likes stories.
And Aaron straightaway starts asking us riddles
which I liked from last time. And the first one was
something like,
MY SIDES ARE TIED TIGHTLY UP.
AND THERE'S NOTHING INSIDE ME.
AND MY HEAD IS VERY STRANGE BECAUSE IT'S
JUST SKIN.
And how are we meant to know that? So we stare
at him.
Then Micah says, "Is it PETE?"
And everyone's laughing. And Aaron has to give
us some clues. And then it's Paolo who gets the
answer which is A DRUM. And everyone claps for
Paolo. Then another riddle goes,
THERE'S A RED LADY IN A ROOM
AND THE DOOR IS ALWAYS OPENING
BUT SHE CAN'T GET OUT.

And this time I get it. I just know the answer
from the way Aaron opens his mouth when he
says it. So I say, "A TONGUE." And that's right.
And then everyone claps for me. Then he asks,
WHAT DO YOU CALL AN EXPLODING MONKEY?
And no one guesses that. But the answer is
A BABOOM!

Then Aaron says things about who he is because
he hasn't met all of us. And he finds out the
names of the ones who are new since last year
like Nathan and Paolo. Then he says we can stay
on the comfortable chairs today instead of going
to work at the tables like normal and he's going
to tell some stories. Then tomorrow we're going to
do writing poems which is what we usually do with
him. Then he starts telling these stories which are
about a fat little man who he told us about last
year. And he's NASRUDDIN. And Aaron knows

loads of stories about him.

And the first one is about when Nasruddin's walking through the market and he's all bruised all over.

And his friend says, "Nasruddin how come you're all bruised up like that?"

Then Nasruddin says back, "A terrible thing happened. My wife threw my clothes down the stairs last night."

And his friend says to him, "But how come YOU'RE bruised up if she threw your clothes down the stairs?"

And Nasruddin says, "The thing is I was wearing my clothes at the time when she did it!"

And then Aaron told us some other stories about him and asked us things about them and got us to try telling one of the stories. And that was it really for the lesson with him. And nobody even did anything wrong except Nathan told Aaron he had a CRAP CAR and Liam told him not to say things like that. And at the end Pete was looking pretty chuffed because there wasn't any trouble or anything.

Then we got to play football because it was BREAK.

And after that we were with Richard for drumming. And as soon as I walked in Richard was looking at me like I had two heads or something. And maybe that's because he was remembering it was me who tried to smash the window at the start of the performance last year. And though he smiled he actually looked like he wanted me to JUST DISAPPEAR IN A PUFF OF SMOKE.

Anyway I just sat down. And the drums and instruments were in the middle and so we were sitting in a circle round them. And I saw the big drum that I was going to play in the performance which is the DJEMBE DRUM.

So I sat there and put it near me.

But Richard says don't touch the instruments yet and Pete tells me to put it back. So I turn round to show Pete I'm going to do it. But straight off Raju gets the djembe drum and puts it near him.

And I say to him, "I'm playing that because it's what I was doing my solo on last year."

And Raju says, "You CHICKENED OUT OF IT last year."

And I'm about to wedge that drum over his little squirt head SO IT WOULD HAVE TO BE SURGICALLY REMOVED.

But Pete saw what I was thinking and he grabbed me and I'm kicking and everything. And Raju's looking as if he never did anything wrong in all his life. And when Pete gets hold of you he gets you round your elbows so there's nothing you can really do because he's just like this great big bear with glasses on.

And he tells me to stop. But I won't. So that's it.
Next thing I'm being carried out.
And I can hear Raju saying, "He's more of a loony than his mum!"
And Pete's saying, "I'm taking you out so you can calm down!"
And that was PRETTY FRIGGING OBVIOUS.
Then when we get to the door I get this glimpse of Barry Holmes. And he's got this sly smile about what's happening LIKE A FAT CAT.
And next thing I'm out in the corridor.
And Liam comes out of his office with his eyes blazing away.
Then Pete leaves me with him and goes back in.
And Liam looks like he had ONE CUP OF COFFEE TOO MANY. And he's not looking exactly CHEERFUL. Though Liam hardly ever looks cheerful which is the opposite of Pete who's so frigging cheerful it almost drives you round the twist.

And he gives me the usual talk which is I can
either PULL MYSELF TOGETHER and IGNORE
RAJU and then go back and do the drumming
with everyone. Or I can sit and think about what's
happening in his office. And I tell him to EFF
OFF and say RAJU'S A LITTLE SQUIRT and the
DRUMMING'S A PILE OF CRAP and probably
some other things as well. And that means next
thing I'm in Liam's office.
And he says to me, "What's making you so angry
Jason?"
And I shrug.
Then he asks again and I say, "THE SMILE ON
BARRY HOLMES'S FAT HEAD."
And Liam nods. And he says he watches everyone
in the class so he knows what goes on. And Barry
and Raju try to wind me up because it's not
difficult to do it which is true.
Then he gets me a glass of water and he says to

me to drink it. So I drink the water.

And he asks me, "WHAT CAN YOU DO TO WIPE THE SMILE OFF BARRY HOLMES'S FACE?"

And I say, "NOTHING."

And he says that's wrong and the right answer is DON'T LET BARRY AND RAJU WIND ME UP. Because I let them do it all the time. Like on Thursday they did it. Then on Friday and now on Monday they did it too. And they LIKE IT when I lose it because IT'S NOT THEM IN TROUBLE.

And then Liam stopped talking at last which was a relief because I already knew everything he said and it took him so long to say it I was starting to get a headache.

And Liam says, "Am I right or am I wrong?"

And he's got this look on his face like he's just made the best speech in all of history. And it's going to change my life. And he knows how to turn cow shit into chocolate.

And I just shrug.

And he's not very happy about that so he tells me to sit and think about what's going on.

And I ask if I can write in my journal book and he says NO I CAN'T.

So I have to sit there and you can hear the drumming in the classroom.

And Liam tries to look like he's doing something important on his computer but you can see he's reading about football transfers on the Internet.

Then he must have talked to Pete about me having a BAD ATTITUDE or something because in the afternoon Pete's not his usual relaxed self again.

And he won't let me just do quiet reading or go on the computer or anything like that.

He says, "We're going to do a science topic just you and I."

So I had to do this work about SOLIDS, LIQUIDS

AND GASES which was as completely boring as it sounds. And the afternoon went past slowly. But I did the work all right. So Pete finally told me to write something in this journal book. And that's this that I've written.

TUESDAY 17th OF MARCH WHICH IS ALSO SAINT PATRICK'S DAY

It's lucky I've even still got this journal book because I nearly threw it in the river. When Mum got back from work yesterday she was in this mood when she says the house is a tip and she's got to clean it. She just gets like that especially if anyone's coming round or something. And the hoover's like a LETHAL WEAPON when she's like that.

So I went down to see if anyone was at the ramp. And I took my journal with me because I wanted to write something better in it than all the BORING CRAP SO FAR which is all about BARRY and LIAM and JON. So I was thinking maybe I was going to write about someone MANAGING A GOOD BMX TRICK. Or a PILE UP ON THE RAMP or something INTERESTING.

But it was already getting dark and a bit rainy. So no one was down there and I didn't write anything. I just sat in the pipe even though it was a bit wet in there. And I looked at all I've written in this and I was thinking what Pete said about writing it being a help. And that's just a PILE OF CRAP because Richard and Aaron coming is just the same as it was last year. IT WAS STILL ME who was the one that got kicked out when everyone else was doing drumming. And I went to the rail by the river and I was going to chuck this thing in the river to prove to Pete he's wrong. But I never did.

I went back. And Mum finally calmed down about cleaning up the flat. So then I put on the telly and she watched a bit with me too.

And that was yesterday and TODAY'S A BRAND NEW DAY as Pete likes singing in the mornings. And it's also SAINT PATRICK'S DAY so on the minibus

Keith was wearing a green shirt because he's Irish. And Barry Holmes said he's going to get drunk tonight. So GOOD LUCK TO HIM if it's true which I DON'T THINK IT IS. And good old Pete was ready and waiting when we got to Heronford. And he says to me when I hang up my coat, "Are you going to try to have a good day Jason?"

And I nod.

So then he says as long as I really DO TRY I can go and do drumming with Richard like normal. Then he's got this thing that we're all COOL in his class. So at breakfast he looks round and says Nazrul passes the COOL TEST because he's got this silky shirt on. And some of the others are cool because of their T-shirts or trainers or something. And me and Barry are cool because we've got cool haircuts. But then Micah's just got his West Ham shirt on. And Pete says can't he do any better than that? But Micah shows him he's wearing

Calvin Klein socks and Pete says that lets him off
the hook because they're cool socks.

Then after breakfast we're with Richard. And he
gives out the instruments. And it isn't me or Raju
who get the DJEMBE. It's Nathan. And I get this
xylophone thing. And Richard says all sorts of
reasons why the person who plays the xylophone is
VERY IMPORTANT.
And he looks at me as if he thinks I'm going to be
very pleased to hear that. But I'm thinking how
can playing a frigging xylophone make anyone
VERY IMPORTANT. And I try the xylophone a bit
and all it does is PLINK PLINK PLONK.
So I'm thinking Richard isn't being completely
straight with me about this.
And Barry and Raju are sort of looking at it as
if it's a girl's instrument or something. And I'm
sitting looking at it too. But I don't want to end

up getting another one of LIAM'S SPEECHES and have Barry Holmes smiling behind my back like AN OVERGROWN CHIMPANZEE. So I don't make any fuss about the frigging xylophone and just join in.

And it wasn't even playing the instruments first but we had to clap this rhythm that went GOOD EGG BAD EGG. Then another that was GOOD APPLE BAD APPLE. And some other different rhythms. Then Richard said we could play our instruments. But as soon as he said that then everyone just started WHACKING THE HELL OUT OF THEIR INSTRUMENTS.

So Pete had to shout to get us to stop and he said we sounded like A HERD OF BUFFALOES AT A RAVE PARTY. And Richard was already a bit grouchy by then. But he got us to play each on our own. And we had two minutes to make up something. So I'm just waiting for Barry and

Raju to start laughing at me when my xylophone
goes PLINK PLINK PLONK. But when I looked
at them they weren't even watching me because
they were trying to do music on their instruments.
And when it was my turn no one laughed in fact.
Then Richard made me do it again. And then he
made me do it another time which was getting
embarrassing. But you could tell he liked what I
did because you can tell when teachers are just
saying you're good and when they're saying it
because it's actually true. And from Richard's face
and the way Pete and Shabana were looking at me
it did seem like what I was doing was good.
And at the end of the lesson it was an all right
lesson. And Richard was looking BRIGHT-EYED
AND BUSHY-TAILED.
And Pete told us what we played sounded FAB
AND GROOVY. And we all got bonuses which
you get if you're good. And they mean if you get

enough you can choose a prize for good behaviour.
And that was that.

Then it was break and even though it was raining
a bit Pete said we could still play football. Then
as soon as we get out there Micah and Barry are
arguing. And Barry says it isn't his turn to go in
goal. But Micah clicks his tongue and says it is.
And I tell Barry it's his turn even though I don't
actually even remember.

Then he shoves his frog face in mine and says for
me to KEEP OUT OF IT BECAUSE IT'S NONE OF
MY BUSINESS.

And I tell him HE CAN BET HIS FAT BUM IT IS
MY BUSINESS. And I was half a second from
NUTTING HIM.

And he says, "DON'T TOUCH ME OR ELSE!"

And I say, "OR ELSE WHAT?"

And he says, "OR ELSE I'LL CUT OFF YOUR ARMS
WITH A SAMURAI SWORD."

Then Pete arrives and takes me away and tells me to keep it together.

And I say, "All right."

Then he goes and talks with Barry too.

And I'm thinking what a lot of crap comes out of BARRY'S BIG GOB because if he's got a samurai sword then I've got curly blonde hair with ribbons in it.

Then Pete says HE'S going in goal. And we can all take shots and NO ONE'S GOING TO SCORE PAST HIM. And he puts on these expressions as if he was this really serious goalie. And I didn't bother about Barry any more because I was trying to score past Pete. And Pete likes rugby more than football because he plays rugby. And you can tell he doesn't know much about football because he supports a completely crap team called CREWE ALEXANDRA which no one ever heard of and is a stupid name for a team anyway. But even so he's all right in goal because he's big and they're not full-size goals or anything.

And every time he saved from one of us he was laughing and saying,

"YOU'RE JUST NOT GOOD ENOUGH!"

And the only one who scored in fact was Paolo. And you can see Pete's happy nothing happened with me and Barry.

Then when we get in the classroom it's time to be with Aaron. But Pete says at the start, "Sorry Aaron. This isn't very professional. But it's what we do in my class."

Then he tells me to get up and stand on the mat. So I do. And I know what's coming. So do all of us. Pete says, "Jason Dooley nearly lost it at break but I asked him to KEEP IT TOGETHER and he did."

Then he jumps up fast and LETS OUT A GREAT
BIG ROAR and CHARGES AT ME and rugby
tackles me right over.
And that's what Pete does to us when he knows you
nearly lost it but you managed not to get in a fight.
And Aaron thinks it's funny and everyone's
laughing.
Then Pete does it to Barry too.
Then he hands over to Aaron.

And Aaron goes straight into saying, "THERE
ARE FOUR DIRECTIONS. NORTH SOUTH EAST
AND WEST. BUT WE ARE GOING IN THE FIFTH
DIRECTION WHICH IS THE DIRECTION OF
STORIES."
Then he starts telling this story which is about a
boy who's about our age. And he's a hunter in a
forest. And he's going through the forest on his
horse. And there's animals in the trees like birds,

foxes and squirrels. And it's in a country that's got a King. And the boy's riding on and on through the forest. And then suddenly everything goes totally quiet. The birds stop singing and even the leaves stop moving.

And he sees there's a feather on the path. It's gold and it's a shiny feather and it's on the path. So the hunter boy stops his horse and he's looking at the feather. And then the horse starts talking because it's a horse that can talk. And it says, "Don't touch that feather or you're going to be sorry if you do because YOU'LL GET IN TROUBLE AND FIND OUT THE MEANING OF PAIN."

So the hunter boy thinks about it.

Is he going to get off the horse and pick up the golden feather?

Or isn't he going to?

Because nobody wants trouble or pain like the horse said there was going to be.

But he's thinking if he picks up that feather and takes it to the King and gives it to him then not even the King has ever got a gold feather like that. So the King's probably going to be happy and give him a big reward for it.

So he keeps thinking. And the feather's there all amazing and golden.

Then he gets off the horse and reaches down on the ground and picks it up.

And that's the beginning of the story.

And Aaron said he's going to tell more of it next time. And Raju said HE SHOULD SAY MORE NOW. But Aaron just laughs and says NO because we're going to do writing. And everyone was complaining about that. But we went to the tables and we did this poem about what the forest was like in the story. We all had to say different things that would be in that forest like birds and oak

trees and beetles and wolves. And Aaron wrote
what we said on the board. Then we had to say
words to describe the different things and words to
say what they were doing. And that was how our
list of things turned into a GROUP POEM. And
Aaron read it out and it was all right.

Then it was dinner. And in the afternoon people
went to their mainstream schools. So like usual on
Tuesday it was me, Barry, Paolo and Raymond
still there.
And nothing happened. Barry went for his
supervision with Liam and seemed like he stayed
there for hours. And Pete wasn't in a WE'RE
GOING TO DO SCIENCE MOOD this time. So he
let me write this.

18th of March Wednesday

Last night Mum got back and said she felt knackered. She'd got some milk and sausages and also orange juice which she doesn't normally get. And she was drinking a big cup of it when she was cooking. Then I went in and asked if it was ready because it smelt good. And when I went in there she quickly put something in the cupboard where she keeps the tins and stuff and she said YES and got me to sit down.

Then she was cooking for a bit more and drinking her juice and when she gives me my plate she starts asking if we did music and stories again at school. So I nodded. And she said, "Well go on! Say what you did!" So I tried remembering and then I thought of the GOOD EGG BAD EGG thing. So I showed it. And it was just normal what I did. But then Mum was laughing for some reason. And I don't know why. And she was trying to stop but she couldn't stop just because I did this little clapping rhythm and said GOOD EGG BAD EGG. Then she said, "Sorry it's just funny." But I still don't know what was so funny. So I just ate my sausages.

Then this morning I had to wake her up instead of her waking me up because Mum overslept. And I don't know when she last did that. She used to do it but she doesn't do it now. And I know why it was because I looked in the cupboard and there was this big bottle of Bacardi there by the tins and loads of it was gone. So that's what she was putting in her juice. But anyway she was saying sorry for oversleeping. And I just got ready in time for the minibus.

Then off we went. And when we got to Barry's house he wasn't coming to school. His mum told Keith he was ill with a headache. So maybe he

DID GET DRUNK last night like he said. Or more likely it was from having to listen to Liam all the afternoon.

Anyway no Barry on the minibus was good news for me. Then we had Aaron first. And so that meant he was going to tell the next bit of the story about the hunter boy. But first he asked questions that got us to remember what happened yesterday in the story. So Nazrul said about who THE HUNTER BOY was. And Micah said about THE HORSE. And I said about the ANIMALS in the forest. Then even Raymond who's never got a question right in his life remembered about how everything WENT QUIET. And Nathan said about THE GOLD FEATHER. And Paolo said how he PICKED THE FEATHER UP. So everyone remembered it all and Aaron's looking pretty pleased with himself about that.

Then he carries on. And he says when the boy picks up the feather he goes off riding on his horse straight to where the King lived in a palace. And he goes in and the King's on a big chair at the end of this long palace room.

So the hunter boy goes up to him and gives him the feather. And the King says, "Thank you. That feather is from a bird called THE FIREBIRD." And then he says some more. He says, "But Hunter Boy a feather isn't enough of a present for a King. If you can get a feather of the firebird then you can get me the WHOLE bird. So go and get the whole of THE FIREBIRD. And if you get it I'll give you a reward. And if you don't my sword I've got is going to cut your head off."

Then the hunter boy isn't too pleased because he thought the King was going to give him something good for a reward. But in fact all the King said was he's got to do something else or he's going to get his head cut off and die.

So the boy walks out of the palace room. And his horse is outside and it says to him. "I told you if you pick up that feather there's going to be TROUBLE AND PAIN. But don't worry because I know what to do. You get a hundred bags of corn and also three strong ropes. Then get up very early in the morning when it's still dark. Then do that and I'm going to show you what you've got to do to catch THE FIREBIRD."

Then Aaron says we're going to leave the story there till tomorrow which is Wednesday.

And what we had to do was write a poem to describe what the FIREBIRD FEATHER would be like. And he said we had to say the colour of it and the size of it and the feel of it and if we got stuck we could ask him.

So we all started writing that. Or some of us did.

Because Paolo can't really write anything. And some of the others can but they didn't try much like Raju. So Shabana and Aaron and Pete went round to help. And Shabana was helping Raju. But even though she was asking lots of questions to help him he kept saying he couldn't write anything because his pencil was too faint. And I saw all he wrote was one line. But because I looked he covered up his paper and told me, "DON'T COPY!"

And I didn't even say anything. And Shabana just tried to carry on helping him. And she said, "What do you think the Firebird feather would feel like if it was in your hand?"

And Raju just slams his pencil down so hard that it broke. Then he crumples the paper up and throws it at the wall and storms off. And Pete tells us just to ignore it and carry on. Then he went out to talk to Raju.

And Aaron said we had ten minutes to finish. But I did mine in less time than that. And it wasn't anything special because I don't know how to do poems. All I said was about the feather being CLEAN and THE GOLDEST COLOUR and LIGHT LIKE A PIECE OF PAPER.

But when Aaron comes round and looks at it he starts OOHING AND AAHING like it's amazing. And I'm thinking HE PROBABLY HAD ME DOWN AS SOME SORT OF DOOFBRAIN WHO WRITES LIKE A CAVEMAN because of trying to throw a flower pot through the window last year.

Then Pete brings Raju back and sits down next to him and Aaron says there's time to hear a few of the poems. And Shabana said what I did was a good poem and I should read it out. But Aaron chooses Nathan first. And he reads his firebird feather poem.

And Raju wasn't listening at all. And Paolo made

a burping noise. And Aaron got angry about that. He said Raju had to sit still and Paolo had to show some respect because Nathan was being brave to read out.

Then he said Raju and Paolo were also going to be reading out their poems some time because we were all going to have to. And when it was their turn everyone was going to listen properly.

Then Nathan did his feather poem again. And also Raymond read his one. And Nathan's was all right because he said the feather LOOKED LIKE IT WAS A BIT OF THE SUN. And everyone clapped when they read out their feather poems. But there wasn't time to get round to me. And that was all right because I wasn't going to do it anyway.

Then after break we went to Richard. And Liam came and sat there again. And at first you could see his eyes were on me. But then he was watching

Raju more because you could see he was still IN
A STROP. And near the start Raju just got up and
went out. Then when Liam went after him he broke
one of A Class's clay tiles that were on the wall in
the corridor.

But we carried on anyway. And Richard gets us to
do this fast drum rhythm. And Nazrul was the one
on the DJEMBE. And it was all right.

Then it was 12.15 and we could have dinner. And
Richard and Aaron went off and it was back to
normal for the afternoon. And when Pete asked
me what I want to do I say I'll write in this journal
which is what I'm doing now.

19th of March Thursday

Last night the doorbell went and I say to Mum, "Who's that?" And she says she doesn't know and tells me to go and see. And I've got this feeling it's going to be Jon. But it wasn't because it was only a woman collecting for children with cancer.

And the sun was shining for once this morning. And Mum was in a good mood because she said Mr Mieri who's her boss from the shop called her and said she was in charge of STOCK-TAKING next week which means counting all the shoes they've got. And it means she's got to get in early but they'll be paying her extra. So she was happy about that.

And when I get on the minibus Keith's smiling. And he says to me, "FEELS LIKE SPRING! LOVELY ISN'T IT?"

Then Barry shows up because he's better. So that spoils things for everyone. But I didn't even pay any attention to him.

And after Barry's we go to Micah's Nan's house because Micah lives with her. And it's over by the park. And there's birds singing. And out the window I can see there's a squirrel running about. So it was like in the story with the hunter boy in the forest with the squirrels and birds there. And when we're sitting waiting for Micah I'm thinking WHAT IF THE BIRDS ARE GOING TO STOP AND EVERYTHING WILL GO QUIET LIKE FOR THE HUNTER IN THE STORY? But that doesn't happen in real life. And the squirrel just disappears up a tree. The birds sing away and the lorries and cars and motorbikes are all going past.

Then at school the sunshine seems to be making

Pete more cheerful than normal. And everyone's in today except Raju's away. And at breakfast Pete says we've got to say what our PERSONAL FAVOURITE SPORT IS. And first Paolo and Micah say FOOTBALL. Then it's my turn and I say BMX RAMP RIDING. And Pete said that SOUNDS COOL which he always says when I tell him about it. Then Raymond says FOOTBALL which is a joke because he doesn't even ever play football at break. And then it's Barry's turn and he says FISHING because his step dad takes him. And I say fishing's NOT EVEN A SPORT because all you do is SIT ON YOUR BUM. Then Barry starts saying IT IS OFFICIALLY A SPORT and anyway you SIT ON YOUR BUM when you ride a bike too so I can shut up. But I say to him, "Cycling's in the Olympics. But whoever heard of anyone being an OLYMPIC CHAMPION OF FISHING?"

And then Barry hasn't got an answer to that.

And his mouth's just hanging open like he's an old lady on the bus. But Pete butts in anyway and tells us it's his turn to say his favourite sport. And everyone knows what that is. BECAUSE IT'S RUGBY because he always goes on about rugby and he's in some team.

But in fact he says SYNCHRONISED SWIMMING. And he says him and Wendy are entering for the Olympics in synchronised swimming. And that's just him joking away because he's a FUNNY MAN. Because then he says RUGBY is really his favourite sport. And he says it leaves you

FIT AS A BUTCHER'S DOG.

And he looks at how we're sitting on our chairs and says we look as if we could do with doing RUGBY TRAINING. And he's going to talk to Wendy about having RUGBY TRAINING instead of breakfast every morning.

But he can go and jump in the lake because

I'm not doing rugby training.

Anyway then Pete says LET'S GET THIS SHOW ON THE ROAD.

So then we do the traditional thing of SAYING OUR FEELINGS. And I give everyone a SURPRISE because I say my feeling is ALL RIGHT.

Then I wanted us to be with Aaron so we could hear what happens now in the story. But it was DRUMMING first. And when I sat down there I asked Richard if I could go on the DJEMBE today. But Richard said NO and he just started giving out the instruments to everyone.

And Barry says to me, "You've got to wait your turn."

And I was going to wait my turn. So I tell him he DIDN'T NEED TO SAY THAT TO ME and I say he's a DUMB FATHEAD. And he says back, YOU'RE NOT SO THIN YOURSELF which is true in fact. Then Richard gets hot under the collar. And he stops everything. And he's shouting out he's not having anyone CALLING PEOPLE NAMES in his lesson. And everyone's listening because Richard looks like now maybe HE'S going to lose it. And Pete's glasses are flashing because you can see he thinks there's going to be trouble. But all I did was say what Barry actually is which is a DUMB FATHEAD. And I'm not even feeling like getting in trouble. And I don't say any more.

Then Richard cools down after a bit. And he carries on giving out the instruments. And he gives Barry a TAMBOURINE which you can see isn't the instrument Barry wanted. Because he takes it and holds it like it's a dead fish or something. But then it gets funnier because Richard asks him to remember what it's called. And Barry looks at it and says A TRAMPOLINE. And that shows what I called him isn't far wrong.

But anyway we did the same fast drumming from yesterday. And it was Raymond who had the djembe drum. And he could do it better than anyone did so far. He could make a really loud sound on it when he hit it with the flat bit of his hand. And his bony elbows were going up and down. And Barry's whacking away at his tambourine. And I've got this COWBELL that didn't look very good when I got it but actually it's noisy when you hit it. And the rhythm got really loud so it felt as though the walls were shaking. Then Shabana even got up and danced. So that seemed as if it made everyone feel better. And Richard liked what we did in the rest of the lesson. And he was looking pretty over the moon for joy by the end of the lesson.

Then after break we were with Aaron. And first he read us some poems. So we listened to that.

And some of them were by him and some of them were by other people. And mainly they were quite funny. Then after that he got us to tell the story of what's happened so far because Barry missed it when he was away. And Micah told the first bit. But he couldn't remember everything that happened with the King at the palace. So I helped him and Aaron let me tell all the rest because I could remember it all. And when I'm saying it I can see how Barry's properly listening to me which is a look I never saw from Barry before. Then Aaron just went straight into carrying on with the story.

And what happens is the hunter boy does everything the horse says he's got to. So he gets the bags of corn and also the strong ropes and early in the morning when it's still dark he's ready. And the horse says they've got to go to this field place behind the palace. Then the horse tells him what to do when they're there. And so the boy scatters out the corn from the bags of corn so it's all on the ground in the field. Then he climbs up a tree that's there and he's hiding in it. Then there's a noise like the sea makes. And the big tree where he is is all shaking and swaying because it's the FIREBIRD coming. And it's this big gold bird that's bright like the sun. And it lands on the ground in the field and starts eating because of all the corn the hunter boy put there.

And the boy stays where he's hiding. But the horse is in the field. And it pretends like it's a normal horse just eating grass so that the firebird won't notice anything. But all the time the horse moves a little bit closer and a little bit closer to the firebird. Then the horse gets so close that it stamps its foot and gets the bird's wing so the firebird can't fly off.

And the boy jumps straight down from the tree
and the bird flaps and tries to fly off as much as
it can. But the boy ties it up with the three ropes.
And that's it.

He gets it and lifts it on his back and carries it to
give to the King. Then he walks to the palace room
where the King is and all these firebird feathers
are falling off on the floor of the palace as he's
coming in. And the King looks happy because he's
got the firebird. And he gives the boy a lot of
coins which are gold coins and silver coins.
And he says, "You can now be an important
person like a SIR." But then he says some more.
He says, "And if you know how to bring me THE
FIREBIRD then it means you're going to know how
to bring me a girl I always wanted to marry. She's a
PRINCESS that lives at the edge of the world. So
you've got to go and get her now. And if you do it
then I'll give you another new reward. But if you

don't do it then my sword is going to cut your head straight off."

And today Aaron didn't stop there. He carried on this time.

He says the boy goes out of the King's room. And he's feeling even worse than he did before because the King's says he's got to do another thing that's even harder or his head's going to be chopped off. But outside his horse is there. And it says to him, "I said if you picked up that feather there was going to be trouble and pain. Well don't worry about that. Just get the King to give you a tent with a gold roof and food and wine that's the best wine in the world. Then get ready because we've got to travel a long way."
So the next day the hunter boy had all the things that the horse said for him to get. And he got

on the horse and started the long journey. And to get to the place they went across more and more different countries. Then they got to the end of the world which was like a beach. And it was called THE LAND OF NEVER. And that was where they were going.

Then Aaron says that's where he's stopping the story today. And Barry pretended to sing the music from Eastenders so he was quite funny for once except Pete and Shabana didn't think so. Then Aaron tells us we've got to write a poem where we're imagining that we're travelling and travelling like the boy is on his horse. And we can choose how we travel. So it can be on a horse or any other type of travelling like a rocket or a submarine or whatever. And he says end every bit with a line saying TRAVELLING TRAVELLING TRAVELLING. Then you write another bit and then put in the line TRAVELLING TRAVELLING TRAVELLING again and keep doing that.

So we did it. And Aaron said we had ten minutes. And Pete sat with Barry because Barry's like Paolo and he can't really write. And I wrote about going in a car and going through a forest and then in a desert. And I was going to have another idea but there wasn't time for it because we had to read out the poems and listen.

And Aaron said who wanted to read out?

And Micah put up his hand. And so did Nazrul. Then Shabana said she wanted to read out Paolo's poem for him and Paolo said, "All right." And Aaron said what about me because I haven't read out anything yet? But I didn't want to do it. And Aaron said that was OK as long as I read something out before the end of the week.

So I said OK.

And Aaron explained this thing which is called

A GOLDEN LINE which means when someone reads their poem then you pick a line which is the one you thought was the best line.

Then we heard the poems. And people clapped and said what golden lines they liked. And Nazrul's poem was about TRAVELLING TRAVELLING TRAVELLING on a motorbike. And I was the one who said a golden line after it. I said I liked the last bit when he said,

"THEN I SKID RIGHT ROUND AND DRIVE MY MOTORBIKE BACK HOME."

And that was what we did.

And when he was giving out bonuses at the end Pete gave me two which was a bit of a record for me.

Then in the afternoon it's just me and Pete who are here as usual because all the others are at their MAINSTREAM. And he says I can go in the quiet-reading corner and read a book or write in my journal if I want. So I'm writing this. Then I'll read a book because at least on Thursdays I can choose any book I want because it's just me here.

Friday 20th

The sunshine didn't last much. This morning it was belting with rain and there was lightning and everything and the sky was like the colour of a bruise on your leg. And it was raining so hard that just from running from the stairs I was already like a drowned rat when I got in the minibus.

And I say to Keith, "FEELS LIKE SPRING! LOVELY ISN'T IT?"

And he says back, "Yeah. Lovely if you're a fish."

Then we did the usual journey round which means getting almost everyone in my class. Except not Raju because his dad brings him. And not Nathan because he lives in the flats next to the school so he walks. And it was so dark out that all I saw when I looked out the window was my reflection looking back.

Then we had Aaron first this time. And Liam came in again so he was sitting there breathing down our necks. And Aaron starts with a riddle. And he says, "I'll carry on with the firebird story if you can get this answer." And it went THE MORE THEY GROW THE MORE THEY GO DOWN. And no one knew that. So Aaron said it might be quite a long wait to get the answer but he didn't mind about that because he didn't have any important plans for the weekend. And we kept trying to get the riddle. Then he gave a clue which was THINK OF THE FOREST IN THE STORY. But no one could get it. Then Aaron said that from the twinkle in Liam's eye he could see that Liam knew it. So everyone looked at Liam and you could see he didn't know it in fact. But you could see him thinking away to get the answer and NOT BE SHOWN UP. And then he said, "The more they grow the more they go down? RABBITS!"

And that was a completely a crap idea . And
everyone laughs. And Aaron tells Liam he's
thinking TOO STRAIGHT AHEAD and with riddles
you've got to think SIDEWAYS to get the answer.
Then he says IT'S NOT EVEN AN ANIMAL. And
some others of us guess things. And Raymond puts
up his hand so quickly that he hits Shabana on her
ear with his elbow and says, "A FOX."
But that's even dumber than Liam because Aaron
just said IT WASN'T AN ANIMAL.
Then it's Pete who puts us out of our misery
because he says ROOTS. And that's right because
THE MORE THEY GROW THE MORE THEY GO
DOWN. So everyone gives Pete a clap. Then Aaron
goes back to the story.

He says the hunter boy and his horse are there at
the end of the world which is called THE LAND
OF NEVER. And he looks out at the sea. And it's

just water and waves going all the way to the sky.
But then out in the sea a boat is coming past. And
it's a gold and silver boat. The oars are gold. And
it's the Princess on the boat.

Then the horse tells the hunter he's got to get the
golden tent. So he quickly puts it up. Then he gets
all the food and wines and things he's got and puts
them in the tent so she can see it all. And then
because the Princess sees it she says that they've
got to row the boat to see what it is. And the
Princess wants to get out on the beach.

And the hunter asks, "Are you the Princess?"
And she says, "Yes."

So he asks her to try the wine and food and they
go in the tent.

And soon they're drinking wine and eating and
talking about where they're from and laughing
with each other. But then the Princess gets tired
because of the wine and she goes to sleep. Then

straight away the hunter folds up his tent and
packs up. And he puts her on the horse. And she's
sleeping all the time. And next thing he's riding like
an arrow to get to the King.

And the journey back is so long it means they go
through 27 countries. And then they get to the
palace. And the King's pleased because he's got the
Princess now. And he gives the hunter boy a lot of
gold and silver coins and then he says, "Now you
are even more important than just SIR."

But then the Princess wakes up and finds out
where she is now. And she asks, "HOW COME I'M
NOT IN MY BOAT WITH SILVER OARS?"

And the King says to her, "I got this boy to bring
you. And now you're going to marry me."

So then the girl is looking sad. And she shakes her
head because she doesn't want to marry that King.
And she says, "I won't get married until I've got
my wedding dress. And it's hidden under a stone

131

out in the bottom of the sea."

So then you know what the King's going to say. And
Aaron asks to say what we think. And Barry says
the answer which is the King says, "ALL RIGHT
THEN HUNTER BOY. YOU GO AND GET THE
WEDDING DRESS." And then the King says, "If you
get it I'll give you a reward and if you don't then
my sword's going to cut right between your head
and your shoulders like lightning. And your head is
going to roll off."

Then Aaron said that was all the story for this
week. And this time people clapped. And we
wanted him to say what was going to happen to
the hunter boy. But he just asked us what we
thought was going to happen. And people said
different ideas.

Like Paolo said the horse would help him because
it was always FAITHFUL.

And Aaron said, "All right let's write some poems about a faithful horse."

And what he asked was for us all to think that we all had our own faithful horse and then write about what it was like. And he didn't say much about how to do it but he said we could put a last line of the poem that started AND WHEN I'M IN TROUBLE... and then say what the horse does. So we did those poems. And I wrote about a faithful horse that was mine. And I said it was GOLD AND YELLOW and IT RUNS THROUGH BURNING FLAMES OR ICE and some other things.

Then I knew what was going to happen because this time Aaron says he wants anyone who hasn't read out a poem to read out their faithful horse poem. And that means it's ME and BARRY and it would be RAJU too but he was away as usual.

And you could see me and Barry weren't in much
of a mood to read out.

But Aaron said all the others were brave and read
out their poems. So now it was our turn. Then he
told people they had to listen and say a golden
line. And he said I was going first. And everyone
was looking. And I said, "Why?"

And Pete said my poem was good and told me to
just get on with it.

And Aaron said, "COME ON BECAUSE THERE
ISN'T MUCH TIME LEFT."

And I did it. And at the end of reading it everyone
was clapping.

And Aaron nods and says, "Perfect sir."

And he asks who's going to pick a golden line from
my poem.

And it's Barry who puts his hand up.

And Barry says he liked the line which said my
horse runs through burning flames or ICE CREAM."

And everyone was laughing at that except Aaron and Liam and Pete and Shabana.

And Barry's sitting there thinking he's so funny that he's SNORTING WITH LAUGHTER. And Liam tells him to GROW UP.

And Aaron gets someone else to pick a proper golden line. And Nathan does it but I don't remember what line he said.

Then Aaron says he really liked my poem and asks me if I'll read it out next week in the performance. So I said all right. Then he says I have to start practising and take it home with me and read it a few times to practise.

Then he says it's Barry's turn.

But Barry says he's not reading his poem because he only wrote two lines.

And Aaron says to him, "Short poems are sometimes the best."

And Pete says Barry should do it because although

it's only two lines they're both good lines. But
Barry's got his pencil and his hand like it's a fist.
And what he does is scribble on the words he
wrote so you couldn't even see them.
And Aaron said that WAS A PITY.
And Pete took Barry out to talk to him.
Then that was break time anyway.

And Liam was by the door when we went out. And
he says to me, "Well done Jason." And I never
heard him say that to me before.
And Barry didn't come out to play football at
break. And when we went back in for drumming
he wasn't around though you could hear him
shouting somewhere.

And what we did in drumming was first this game
Richard showed us called GHOST DRUMS AND
JUNGLE DRUMS. And then we did a song with the

instruments that had lines from all the different
TRAVELLING TRAVELLING TRAVELLING poems
we wrote. And Richard got me to play the music
I did on the xylophone before. So that was part of
the song. And it was easy to do it again.
Then in the middle of that Barry comes in and
he's with Wendy. And she makes him say sorry to
Richard for being late and then he says sorry to
me for being rude about my poem. But I didn't say
anything about that and Richard just gave him
a shaker and told him to join in. And we did the
song a few more times. And that was it.

Then in the afternoon I had my supervision with
Liam which is meant to be on Thursday but it's
different this week because Richard and Aaron
are here. And Liam says how different this week
was from last week and it was much better. So I sat
there and agreed with him in all the right places.

And he gave me my bonuses back which I'd lost
last week. So that was all right except then Liam
tried to tell me I've got to sort things out with
Barry. And he said I was good at ignoring this
week and now I can do even better than that. And
I've got to try and be friends with Barry. Because
he says BARRY'S FRIENDLY AND FUNNY if you
actually chat with him.

But I say to him I'd enjoy CHATTING WITH A
SPONGE MORE THAN I WOULD WITH BARRY
HOLMES.

Then even Liam laughed when I said that.

Then in the classroom Pete let me write this.

And now the lesson's nearly over so he started
tidying things. And when he was doing it he said
to me, "What a shame you had such a good week
Jason."

And I look at him and say, "What?"

And he says, "Well if this week's been very good

then next week's PROBABLY GOING TO BE
VERY BAD."
And that's Pete trying to be funny as usual
because half the time he acts like he thinks we're
in some comedy programme on TV.

Then when I got home I felt all right because the
week was over. So I was looking forward to just
lazing about and watching the football which is
mostly what I do at the weekend.
And Mum got back early and she'd got me some
new trainers from the shop. She said they were for
school because she didn't like me going in my old
ones because they look dirty now. Then she put
the kettle on. And I put on the trainers. And they
were all right. And she asked about school. Then
I told her about Richard and Aaron and us doing
the performance next Friday and that parents
could come. And she said she was going to try

to come. And she did look like she really wanted to come to it. But she always does and she never actually comes. And anyway just then the doorbell went. And she says for me to see who it is. And it's Jon.

He still had his arms plastered up and everything. But he looked better than before. Like he was shaved and had this white shirt on. And he smiles this smile with one side of his mouth and he says to me, "All right Jacey? Your mum in?"
And I'm going to tell him she's out but then he just walks in past me anyway. And I follow him in the kitchen. Then Mum's asking if he's all right. And she says she'll make him a tea. But he doesn't want it. And he tells her he's back at work and he's settled up the rent with his landlord. And Mum's happy about that.
Then Jon says, "Listen what I came round for

was to say THANK YOU for helping me out. And
I thought I'd get you a Chinese takeaway. How
about that?"

And he smiles so his blue eyes are looking shiny.
And Mum says, "All right."

Then Jon goes back out down to the takeaway
place to get it.

And when the door's shut I say to Mum, "You said
Jon wasn't coming back here."

And she says, "Don't worry about it because
he's not staying this time. He's just getting us a
Chinese."

And then she was saying how Chinese takeaway is
my favourite which is true. And there was nothing
much I could say back to her because I didn't
know what to say.

But I know Jon was sometimes this smiley bloke
who told jokes and showed up with flowers for
Mum and things that made you think he was all

right. But I also know a boy at my old school told me about a fight he heard about Jon having. And Jon broke this man's jaw and knocked out four teeth with one punch. And all he was doing was picking up Mum when she worked at ASDA. Then when he got back you should see the takeaway he got. Because there was SWEET AND SOUR CHICKEN and SPARE RIBS and RICE. Then there were SPRING ROLLS and this DUCK STUFF and another type of rice I never had and also TOFFEE BANANA.

And he's got a bottle of wine for him and Mum. And they start drinking it and Mum says it's lovely. And Jon sits there with his broken arms resting on the table and because he's in a good mood that meant Mum started getting in a good mood herself.

And the Chinese was all right especially the SPARE RIBS which is what I always like. And Mum was

saying he put too much on her plate and she's got
to watch her weight and how she used to be able
to STOP A MAN IN HIS TRACKS but now she's got
fat so she can't. But Jon said, "You still stop me in
my tracks."
And even though we all ate loads there was still
some left. And they got through most of the wine.
Then Jon lit up a fag. And then he did this thing
where he showed us how you can set fire to your
own hand by putting gas from his lighter on it and
then setting fire to it and the flame doesn't hurt
you because the flame goes up.
Then Mum started remembering about this time
when they went to a fancy dress party. And she
said she was SNOW WHITE and then Jon was a
KANGAROO. And both of them were laughing
about the party because on the way back the
POLICE STOPPED JON. And the police said they
were after a man who just robbed a shop dressed

like a rabbit. And Jon was telling them he was A KANGAROO. But the police said he was A RABBIT and they wouldn't let him go. And Mum and him are falling about laughing about the story. And Jon said, "Those coppers were HOPPING MAD weren't they?" And then Mum was laughing at him because he was joking. And Jon says, "They shouldn't have JUMPED TO CONCLUSIONS should they!"

And it was quite funny but not so funny as they were thinking it was.

Then they were chatting on like they were best old friends. And after eating I didn't even feel like sitting there. And there wasn't anything I wanted to watch on telly so I came here in bed which is where I'm writing this.

I just went to sleep after I wrote that. But I woke up after a bit. And Jon's still here because him and Mum were still talking. They were in the living room and you couldn't hear what they were saying. But I lay there and listened and you could tell Jon wasn't going even though Mum said he would. Because I heard her getting things out the cupboard where she keeps the sheets. So she was getting covers for him to sleep here.

Then she went to bed like normal and I heard the springs on the sofa because Jon was lying there.

And I couldn't sleep after that. And neither could Jon from the sound of it. You could hear this CREAK CREAK CREAK from the living room every few minutes that meant he was still awake. And I could smell smoke from him smoking.

Then after ages it sounded like he got up.

And he did because there were footsteps in the hall.

So I'm thinking WHAT'S HE UP TO? Because it

sounds like he's going in Mum's room. And I was right. The sound of the door was the sound of her door opening.

Then I didn't know what was going on. But I wasn't going to just lie there. I was saying to myself if Jon was in Mum's room and she starts telling him to get out then I'm going to go there to help her get rid of him.

So I nerved myself to get up. And then I got up. And the lights were off. But a bit of light was coming from the street so you could see a bit. And there were just crumpled covers on the sofa. So Jon was in Mum's room. And I went near her door and it was just quiet. I couldn't hear anything. I even felt maybe Jon was standing and listening the same as me. And I was thinking what if he comes out and finds me there? But also what if Mum needs help? So I wasn't going to go back to my room. I went in the bathroom. And I didn't put the light on. I just waited there so I could hear in her room.

And I'm in there standing sort of behind the door. And that's when I hear her voice.

"What you doing?" she says.

And Jon's voice says, "I couldn't sleep. I was cold on my own."

And I couldn't hear what Mum said. All I could tell was she started speaking quieter and then that made Jon drop his voice too.

I don't know how long went past. But she wasn't telling him to get out or anything. And if she was just letting him stay it must mean she didn't mind him being there. So I was standing in the dark and thinking about Mum and Jon maybe getting back together and what was going to happen if that happened.

Then the bedroom door opened.

And first I think GOOD Mum told him to get out.

So he's going back on the sofa.

But actually his footsteps came straight where I was.

So I snapped out of what I was thinking and opened the cupboard where Mum puts towels. And I ducked in it. And I was still shutting the door when the light came on. And the cupboard door's made of bits of wood with gaps between. So I could see it was Jon. He was wearing a vest and boxer shorts and also carrying his trousers.

And he gives this little yawn. He takes a look at himself in the mirror. Then he walks back to the door like he's going out again.

But actually he LOCKS THE DOOR.

So we were both locked in now.

Then he sits on the edge of the bath and he's so close I know if I make one sound he'll hear where I am.

And when he's sitting there he sort of looks about.

He stares at the laundry basket which is an old one from a hotel Mum's got. And he looks at her make-up things on the shelf. Then he looks round where I am. And I stay completely still. But Jon's eyes are looking right where I am.

And it's as if light's coming through the gaps and he can see me. And I'm sure he's about to shout and kick open the door or something.

But he doesn't. He just looks away and gives his shoulders a little roll.

Then he gets something out of his trouser pocket. It's like a tub of talcum powder or something like that. But he opens it and tips out what's in it. And it's stuff for taking heroin like him and Mum used to.

And then that's what Jon does. He gets a spoon and tips in some powder stuff out of a little bag. Then he mixes it with water in the spoon.

And he's looking more careful than I ever saw Jon

look. Then he gets his lighter and lights it under the spoon so it starts making a sort of sizzle sound. And I'm hardly even breathing in case he hears. Then I can see he's going to inject it like they do when they give you an injection. He puts a needle in the spoon and sucks the drugs into it. Then he shakes it and then he pushes it in his skin in his arm just near where it's plastered. And from his face he doesn't even feel it hurt. But he pushes it right in deep because there's blood making the drugs in the needle thing go red. Then he pushes it and the drugs go in him.

And he lets go. And he leaves the needle just hanging out of his skin. He doesn't move. He just breathes and sits there for a bit. Then at last he takes out the needle from his arm. And he puts the spoon and things back in the tub and then in his trouser pocket just pretty much as if nothing happened. Then he sits down a little bit more. And then he gets up and unlocks the door. The light goes off and he's gone.

And I'm listening to see where he goes.
But I don't hear Mum's door opening again.
There's a sound of him lying down back on the sofa.
But I wait a bit in the dark in the cupboard and I'm thinking all Jon's been saying about not taking any more drugs and living his happy life is just him TALKING CRAP.
And what happens if I go in Mum's room and tell her what I saw?
What's she going to do then if I do that?
And then what would Jon do?
I can remember lots of times when she was trying to kick jon out of the flat. And all he did was sit on the sofa and when she said for him to get out he just shook his head.

Because how can Mum actually throw him out?
All she ended up doing was shouting at him more
and more. And when she was shouting was usually
when Jon lost it with her.

So I'm thinking I'll wait till the morning. Then
when he goes and it's just me and Mum in the
flat again I can talk to her about it without any
fight starting. Then she can just NOT LET HIM IN
AGAIN if he comes back another time.

So I get out the cupboard and I'm trying to be
quiet. But there's some bathroom cleaner stuff
and it knocks over.

So I stop and I listen.

But I just want to get quickly out of there to
my room now. So I just go. And right when I'm
stepping out the bathroom I hear the springs on
the sofa.

And that's it. I know Jon heard me.

I look down at the living room thinking I'm going

to see his eyes looking at me.

But he isn't looking.

I can just see the shape of him under the covers.

He must have just been turning over.

And I get back to my room. And I try to go
to sleep.

But I'm WIDE AWAKE.

So I got this journal from where I keep it. Because
I've got a place for it on the shelf between the
football books my Grandad gave me when I was
little. And no one can notice it there once I put it
there. And I've written this about what happened.

Saturday

I never got a chance to talk to Mum in the
morning. I woke up too late and it meant she'd
already gone to work. And the TV was on. So I
knew Jon was still around. And I tried to go back
to sleep because I wanted to wake up and find he
wasn't here any more. But the TV went on and on
and I couldn't sleep anyway. So I got up.

Jon's covers and things were folded but he was on
the sofa watching MTV. And he looked sort of
slowly up at me and nodded but didn't say much
for a moment.
Then what he says is, "Another day another
doughnut Jacey."
And I nod and walk in the kitchen.
And there's a note Mum's left with some money to
get chicken and chips for lunch and it says,

BACK AT THE USUAL TIME AND I'LL COOK A NICE MEAL FOR US BECAUSE IT'S MY TURN!

I looked at that and I didn't know if US meant me and her or Jon too.

Then I put some toast on. And I didn't want to say anything to Jon so he'd get the message to clear off. And my bag for school was down on the floor and I looked in it and got my HORSE POEM and put it on the table so I could read it like Aaron said to do.

And the songs on the telly went on. I had my toast. And Jon didn't say anything. And I didn't really look at the poem much but I put it there as if I was.

Then the sofa creaks and it's Jon getting up and he

comes in. And straightaway he looks down at the poem and after a bit he asks, "Did you write this?" I nod and Jon picks it up. Then he reads it.

And he's got this look not laughing or anything which is what I thought he was going to do but staring and chewing because he's got chewing gum. Then he suddenly looks at me and says almost shouting, "VERY GOOD BOY!" Then he tells me, "There's a game starting. You gonna watch?" And I say, "I'm having breakfast."

And he doesn't say anything more. He goes back and the sofa creaks and he changes channels to see the build up to the match.

And I put my poem back where it was in my bag.

And after the usual talk about teams and everything on the telly you can hear the game starting and Jon's sitting watching. And I finish my toast and it looks a lot like Jon's not going anywhere. He's just watching the game. But I'm not sitting in the kitchen all day. So I get up and go in the living room. And Jon starts talking about the match as if it's normal he's sitting there watching it. And he says there's some midfielder who started the game running about like A ROTTWEILER. And he tells me to watch.

And I watch a bit. But it's only Fulham against Sunderland and I'm not too bothered about it. And Jon doesn't look so bothered himself because he yawns. Then he looks round and says, "You hear the one about the man who takes his rottweiler to the vet?" I shake my head.

Then he says, "The vet says WHAT'S THE PROBLEM? And the man tells him I THINK MY DOG'S CROSS-EYED.

So the vet picks it up and looks at the dog's eyes. Then he says I'M GOING TO HAVE TO PUT IT DOWN.

And the man says WHAT? YOU'RE GOING TO PUT DOWN MY ROTTWEILLER JUST BECAUSE IT'S CROSS-EYED?

And the vet says, NO! BECAUSE IT'S HEAVY!"

And maybe it was a funny joke. But I wasn't in the mood for it. And Jon turns down his mouth and chews a bit.

Then he says, "You look like a TURKEY ON CHRISTMAS EVE Jacey! Sit down! Watch the match!"

Then he looks back at the football. But I say I'm not interested.

Then he says, "Well if you're not watching it you can do me a favour instead. I was going to ask you after anyway."

And he gets this envelope out from his pocket and looks at me and says, "It's important. Take this up to the leather shop at the traffic lights. You know the place. LEATHERSTOP AND SHEEP SKINS.

You've got to give it to Ali Khan. He's the boss.
Tell him it's from me. And don't give it to anyone
except him because this is important."
I knew the place but I wasn't going up there for
Jon. I just stared at the football.
And Jon says, "Here. I'm talking to you. This has
got to get to Ali Khan at the leather shop."
But I shake my head.
Then in a flash Jon says, "Who are you shaking
your head at? DON'T FRIGGING SHAKE YOUR
HEAD AT ME!"
And he looks at me like he used to look.
His lips are tight right on his teeth. And when I
see him like that it makes me straightaway think
about all the worst stuff he did.
And he goes, "D'you want me to make you
do it?"
And I lean away but his hand grabs my face so
the plaster's squashing in my nose and his thumb's

under my chin and his fingers are pressing near my eyes and I can't move my face away from him.

And he shouts, "D'YOU WANT ME TO MAKE YOU DO IT?"

I say, "NO!"

Then he says, "Then what you doing shaking your head at me? And why are you moping round like you can't wait for me to go? If your mum says I can stay I CAN. And you can show a bit of respect to a guest!"

And as he says it his eyebrows squeeze together as if he's sad.

"THIS IS IMPORTANT!" he says.

And I say, "THEN WHY DON'T YOU DO IT?"

And I don't know what he's going to do then.

But actually what he does is smile. And he says, "I'll tell you exactly why Jacey. Now you're such a big boy I'll tell you a BIG BOY'S STORY. These broken arms I got weren't any accident. Me and this Ali Khan had a bit of a run in after some business I did for him. So I started working with someone else. And he doesn't like that. And also I owe him a bit of money. And because it was taking me a while to pay he sends his boys round. And they ask for what I owe. But I haven't got it. So they THROW ME OUT A THIRD FLOOR WINDOW. And THAT WASN'T MUCH FUN. In fact it smashes up my arms like this. And they just leave me on the ground and tell me I've got a week to get the money or next time they'll make sure I'M AN EFFING VEGETABLE FOR THE REST OF MY LIFE. And that was three weeks ago. So I don't want to run into them till Mr Ali Khan says WE'RE STRAIGHT. So that's why I'm sending you Jacey. Because right now I don't know if tomorrow I'm going to be in a frigging wheelchair, a frigging coffin or what." And he's still got his fingers on my eyes so I can't move. And he holds out the envelope and says, "Here. End of story." But I still don't take it.

Then he pushes his fingers in my eyes.

And it hurts so much I think I'm going to throw up. And he says, "I CAN POP YOUR EYES RIGHT OUT OF YOUR HEAD IF YOU WANT!"

And I say, "DON'T!"

And he stops and then he says, "THEN YOU'D BETTER POP OUT LIKE I TELL YOU!"

And I couldn't do anything. You could see it on Jon's face. He was going to make me do what he told me. I wasn't going to stop him not even with Barry Holmes's SAMURAI SWORD.

So I took the envelope.

And he lets go and says, "I've been watching you Twinkle Toes. You think you're the big man now don't you? Well if you try to act big with me you're gonna regret it!"

Then he looks back at the match. And I go in the kitchen with this lonely feeling I used to get when Jon made me do things before.

And I pick up the money Mum left for chicken and chips.

And I hear Jon say, "Ali Khan. LEATHERSTOP AND SHEEP SKINS. And I want to know what he says."

Then when I'm getting my bike he looks round and says, "And this is between ME AND YOU. I'm not having your mum running to the police again. So NOT A SQUEAK TO HER. Or I swear I'll kick the living daylights out of you."

I didn't say anything back. I just went.

And Jon shouts, "OFF YOU GO SOLDIER!"

I bang the door and carry my bike down the steps. It's sunny out there. And the road's busy up by the

shops because it's Saturday. And I scoot through
the people and round the cars that are stuck at
the roundabout.

Then I ride along the wrong side of the road
past the new flats they're finishing. And the
LEATHERSTOP shop's just up on the corner by
the lights.

I take my bike right in and put it by the door.
There's lots of racks of coats and things in there.
And the heating's blowing hot air about. And it all
stinks of leather. And a man comes over like he
doesn't much like the look of me. And that's all
right because I don't much like the look of him.
And I just say, "I've got something for Ali Khan."
And he says, "What?"

And I say, "I've got something from Jon."
Then the man says like he's a parrot, "From Jon."
And I nod and say, "For Ali Khan."
And he says to wait and goes up some stairs.

Then he comes down and says, "He's up there."

So I go up the stairs. And there's a door at the top that's open a bit. And I'm imagining what Ali Khan's going to be like. I'm thinking it's going to probably be some giant bloke all dressed in leather or something.

Then I go in and it's an office and there's this little bloke with bulgy eyes wearing a tracksuit. And there's a telly on and it's a cartoon. That one about THE PINK PANTHER. He's staring at it with his legs stretched out and smiling at the cartoon. And he holds up a hand to say to stay quiet. And there are photographs on the walls which I can see are of him shaking hands with different people or with their arms round each other. Then the music comes on because THE PINK PANTHER'S finishing.

So Ali Khan looks round and looks at me and then

says, "What can I do for you young man?"

So I say, "Jon sent this."

And I give him the envelope. Then he opens it. And I could see it was money in there. And Ali Khan doesn't move from how he's sitting. But he counts the money quickly like people do in films.

Then he looks at me with the money just lying there on his legs.

And he says something like, "So who are you? Jon's PUBLIC RELATIONS OFFICER?"

And I say back, "I just know him."

And the man nods. Then he scratches his chin without saying anything. Then he goes, "So Jon's sending me kids is he? IN THE NAME OF GOD. I've got a boy your age." And he looks a bit more at the telly. And while he watches it he says, "What have I done? Scared the pants off him?" Then he starts laughing a bit. And he looks round and looks right at me and he says, "Jon did some good business for me. But he broke the rules you see. He didn't pay me my share of the thing. And he thought he could get away with it as if he was one of God's chosen. And then he started doing business with some African chap who's stupid enough to think he can compete with me. And I don't let these things pass."

He seemed like he thought I was going to say something back. But all I wanted to do was get out of there. Then he pressed the remote control and the telly went off. And everything was quiet. And he looked at me with his eyes almost bulging right out of his head. And he says, "Do you like SPORTS?"

I shrugged.

And he says, "As you can see I do." And he waved his hand so I looked at the photos on the walls. "That's me with the CRICKET WORLD GREATS." And he said the names of players that were in the photos although I'd never heard of any of those names.

Then he starts going on about how in sports you PLAY ROUGH BUT YOU PLAY WITH RULES. And I'm starting to think I'd rather be in Liam's office than get a frigging lecture about cricket from this bloke.

But he says, "I'm in the import and export business. It can get dirty I admit it. But there are rules and I keep them. And people who work for me keep them too."

Then he went on about Jon breaking the rules and he said, "He's a cheat. And you know what else he is? He's A COWARDY CUSTARD!"

Then Ali Khan nodded as if that's the end of the conversation.

Then he said again "A COWARDY CUSTARD", as if he was just saying it to himself.

And I told him, "I'm going."

"Good," he said back. "May God richly bless you."
Then he looked down at the money on his legs and
he says, "And listen tell Jon three things. Tell him
WE'RE QUITS. And tell him I'm a family man and
I don't like youngsters being sent round here. And
tell him to steer clear of the African or my boys
will be after him. And next time I swear to holy
God THEY'LL CUT HIM IN HALF LIKE THE RAT
HE IS!"
I went and I heard the sound when you press the
remote control and the TV comes back on. Down
the stairs I got my bike and headed off.

Then I'm coming back down the road. And I'm not
in a hurry to go back and sit around with Jon. And
I don't mind if he's stuck there watching Fulham
against Sunderland not knowing if I did what I was
meant to with the money.
So I go and get the chicken and chips that Mum

left me money for.

And I sit on a bench by the shops eating and watching all the people doing their normal Saturday stuff. And I look over at our flats. And I remember what it was like when Mum finally got rid of Jon from our flat when she told the police about him selling drugs. He never showed up after that except sometimes I had dreams with him in it. And also I kept thinking someone I saw in the street was him. But it never was. It was always someone who just looked a bit like him.

And anyway I had my chicken and chips. Then I pedal round the back of the shops to the river. And there's people there this time. Like Ashraf and Imam from my old school who are all right. But I didn't ride on the ramp or anything. I just sit there on the benches and it took my mind off things because I was remembering when Imam tried to do a wheelie but he crashed into this silver van!

And Ollie shows up and his mum's with him. And he came talking to me and says he's got a new trick he can do called A BAR SPIN. But he only half manages it after trying about five times. And his mum's saying, "OLLIE! BE CAREFUL!"

And you can see Ollie wishes she'd just disappear. But she won't. And after a bit she says to him IS HE THIRSTY and does he want one of these little apple juice drinks she's got in her bag? And you can see he doesn't want her to ask him that either because he tells her he doesn't want it.

So she says do I want one and I say, "All right". And she says it's ORGANIC. And that's all right. I sit and drink it. And she starts going on about why she's there with Ollie. Because she says SHE WASN'T BORN YESTERDAY and she knows there are drug dealers sometimes at skate parks and she

doesn't want Ollie to get involved with that.
Then she asks if I ever saw anyone with drugs
down there. And I said NO which is true.
And anyway what was I meant to tell her? That
half an hour before I was watching The Pink
Panther with the biggest drug-dealer round here?
So I just drink the juice and hang about. But then
it's getting on for five. And I know Mum will be
getting back. And I wanted to see what happened
in the football. So I went back.

And Mum wasn't back. There wasn't any sign of
Jon either. But the bathroom door was shut. And
he was in there because you could hear he was in
the bath. So I put on the telly to see the football
results and Jon shouts out from the bathroom,
"DID YOU GIVE IT TO ALI KHAN?"
And I tell him I did it. And he comes out of the
bathroom and is asking WHAT KEPT ME? And

WHAT DID ALI KHAN SAY? And I told him about it and how Ali Khan said they were quits and all of what Ali Khan said.

And when I've said it all Jon looks happy about it. And as they're saying the Scottish football results he's looking at the telly as if he's not really looking at it. Then he points a finger at me and he says, "NOT A SQUEAK!"

And I just watch the telly because they're starting the match reports.

Then there's a sound of Mum coming back. And she's got shopping she puts in the kitchen. And she asks if we're all right. And I look round and nod. And she's putting a big bottle of Coke in the fridge. And she says she's got all the things to make us roast beef with all the trimmings which sounds all right to me.

But then what happens is after the football reports

are over Jon starts saying to Mum that instead
of staying in the two of them could go out for a
drink.

And he says he's got some money. And he asks her
when was the last time she went down the pub
they always went to? And he says it's great down
there because her old friends are always there.

And Mum doesn't look very sure about it. But she
says to me she hasn't been out for a drink for a
long time which is true.

And I just shrug and change channels on the telly.

And Mum says it's just going to be a quick drink.

And there's some wildlife programme about bears
on. So I start watching it.

And Mum asks IS IT ALL RIGHT?

And I could tell she wanted to go out because she
never did these days.

So I said, "Yeah."

Then she was changing into clothes for going out

174

and in the bathroom putting on make up. And her
and Jon were looking happy about it. Then Mum
makes some chicken soup and cheese on toast
for me.

And Jon's standing looking at the thing about the
bears. And he's joking with Mum about cooking
a tin of soup instead of roast beef with all the
trimmings like she said. And Mum says she's going
to make the roast tomorrow. Then she brings me
my soup so I can eat on the sofa. And she asks if
I'm going to be all right.

And I say, "Yeah. Fine."

And I start eating my soup.

And Jon puts on his jacket. But Mum waits a bit
and she's looking at the programme about the
bears.

And Jon says, "If I had to I could survive out
there in the wild with nothing except a knife."

And Mum says, "And A PACKET OF FAGS."

And Jon laughs a bit and nods and says, "And
A LIGHTER."

Then they go. And I've got the place to myself.
And I ate my soup. And usually if I'm on my own
I sit and watch what's on the telly. But now I'm in
my room instead. And I'm writing all this
that happened.

Sunday

I heard them come in. The quick drink they went
for turned out not to be very quick in fact because
you could hear that birds were singing when they
got in. And Jon sounded like he was pretty off his
head because he was starting singing too. And
Mum quickly told him to shut up. But I heard her
laughing as well.

Then after a bit I heard the sound of her bedroom
door and then it went quiet. And I don't know
if it was just her in her room or her and Jon.
But I'm lying there half awake and there's a
mixture of different dreams and things in my head.
And one of them is remembering when Marie took
me when I had to go to the home last year. I was
carrying my stuff down from the flat to her car.
And that was the worst sort of sad feeling I
ever had.

And when we got to the home Marie stayed for a bit but then she had to go. So I was left there on my own with this woman who worked there asking questions that seemed to go on for about 900 years.

And then when she finally stopped she said did I want to ask her anything?

And I asked HOW LONG WAS I GOING TO BE THERE? And she said that was the one question she couldn't answer. And that made me feel like I wasn't ever going back home.

And the flat went completely quiet for a long time. So it sounded like Mum and Jon were sleeping now. But I was still awake. So I just lay there and I was deciding I'M GOING TO WAKE UP EARLY AND I'M GOING TO TELL MUM EVERYTHING ABOUT JON. LIKE HOW I SAW HIM TAKING DRUGS AND ABOUT HOW HE MADE ME GO

TO THE LEATHER SHOP AND HOW HE ALWAYS
USED TO DO THAT BEFORE.
And I didn't care what Jon was going to do when I
told her that.
BECAUSE I DON'T WANT THINGS TO GO BACK
LIKE THEY WERE BEFORE.

And then I go back to sleep.

And I do wake up early and I get up straightaway.
And Jon's there sleeping on the sofa. So I'm
glad he's not in Mum's room. He's stretched out
there like he's dead. And I'm thinking DOESN'T
LOOK LIKE WE'LL BE GETTING JON'S FAMOUS
SUNDAY FRY-UP TODAY.
And I go in the kitchen and put on some toast.
But I make sure I'm quiet and I don't wake up Jon
because I want to talk to Mum before him and say
what I decided to say to her.

Then I eat my toast. And I wait. And it's a long time. But I hear Mum's door. So she's awake. And she goes in the bathroom. And I'm waiting for her to come out. And Jon hasn't moved at all from how he was when I got up. And Mum takes a long time in there. So I go to see. And she's got the door open. She's sitting on the toilet not using it but sitting on it just with the lid down.

And I say is she all right? And it's like she heard but she didn't listen.

And then I know what's happened.

I remember what that slow look on her face was like. It was when she took drugs. I remember it so many times that I could just tell. And she looked at me and smiled. But there wasn't anything in her eyes. It was because she'd taken heroin again. So what was the point of telling her I knew Jon had taken the stuff? She knew. She kept smiling then wanting to put her arm round me.

BUT I DIDN'T WANT HER ARM ROUND ME OR
TO TALK TO HER LIKE THAT.

And she could tell. I didn't even have to say
anything.

She looked at me and said, "Don't worry Jason."

And it was like she was sitting there but not all of
her was really there.

And she says she's going to cook something special.
Then she gets up and goes out.

And I lock the door shut. And I'm sitting there
thinking about if Mum goes back to taking drugs.
And then it will be like before. Half the time it
means she's miles away because she's taken the
stuff. Then half the time she's in the worst mood
you ever saw her because she wants to take it.

AND BOTH WAYS SHE WASN'T LIKE MY
MUM.

And I'm sitting with my head on my hands.

And I didn't want to just do that. But I didn't want to do anything else either. Because I remember Mum saying how she wouldn't touch drugs ever again. Never in her life. And I don't know how long I was in there. But all I can think about is Mum going back like she was. And thinking about it was even making me shake.

And I wanted JON TO EFF RIGHT OFF because Mum never took drugs before he was around.

And she stopped when she got rid of him.

And IT'S HIM that always got it for her.

Then I hear his voice. So he's awake now. And I go out. And he's lying there. And I feel like I'm just going to walk there AND HIT HIM SO HARD IT CRACKS HIS SKULL.

But he looks at me. And his little eyes are looking right at me. And I don't do it.

And he says, "You all right Jacey?"

And I nod.

And he says, "Have you got something to say? Eh?" And I just look and he says, "SAY IT OR EFF OFF AND LET ME GO BACK TO SLEEP".

And I don't say anything. I go in the kitchen. And Mum's in there cooking.

Then there's a creak as Jon turns over. Then he punches the sofa and turns back the way he was and says, "IT'D BE MORE COMFORTABLE SLEEPING ON TOP OF AN EFFING CROCODILE!"

And in the kitchen Mum's getting the food-mixer out. And Jon shouts out does she have to make all the noise. Then she tells him she's making the roast beef and doing Yorkshire pudding with it and everything.

And Jon looks at his watch and shouts, "IT'S EFFING NINE O'CLOCK IN THE MORNING!"

And Mum says doing a roast with all the trimmings takes a long time.

And Jon tells her it doesn't. Then he starts saying

about how he knows because he trained to be a chef. And he turns over again with the covers over his head.

Then Mum turns on the food mixer.

And Jon straightaway shouts, "TURN THAT OFF!"

And Mum tells him, "SHUT UP!"

Then Jon's biting his teeth and coming in the kitchen. And he says, "DON'T YOU GET BITCHY WITH ME!"

And it's like it used to be. And I don't want to hear it.

And I shout at him, "WHY DON'T YOU JUST EFF OFF!"

And Jon looks at me and says, "THAT'S THE BEST EFFING IDEA I'VE HEARD ALL YEAR!"

Then he's getting on his trousers.

And Mum s saying, "I'm cooking roast beef for us!"

But Jon's looking around for his jacket.

And he finds it and he says, "Eat it with Jason!

He's the big man of the house now!"

And he says it again shouting, "EAT IT WITH JASON!"

Then the door slams and he's gone.

And I think that's good. Except what happens is Mum turns on me. She says why do I have to get involved? She says if she's arguing with Jon it's not to do with me. And I tell her IT IS. And I kick a chair so it falls backwards and shout at her and say I know she took some heroin again. Then she's saying how it isn't a problem. And it was just a little treat. And she's got herself together enough to take just a little bit just at the weekend without getting hooked like before.

And I tell her she said to me SHE WASN'T EVER TAKING IT AGAIN. NEVER.

And then she says, "I just ..." And she never finishes what she's saying. And she picks up the chair. And I walk out and put on the telly and

there's some crap like CHARLIE AND LOLA on
but I just sit and watch it.

And Mum doesn't say any more. She just carries
on cooking what she's making and putting
everything on the table. And it's roast beef then
roast potatoes and Yorkshire pudding and peas
and everything like she said. Then she says it's
ready and tells me to come and eat. But it's like
eleven in the morning and I wasn't hungry. So I
didn't move. I sat watching the crap that was on
the telly. And Mum tried getting me to go there
another time. But I didn't go.

So she sits there with all the food just on her own.
And she's staring straight ahead and eating like
she's really hungry. And after a bit she finishes.
And I still don't say anything.

Then she stays in the kitchen and she starts
cleaning everything. I looked and saw. She was
slowly and carefully washing up everything and

putting it away. And wiping the kitchen tops and the top of the cooker and then the sink. Then she comes out and she says to me she hardly slept last night so she's going to have a lie down.

And I was sick of what was on the TV. So I'm in my room writing this.

Monday 23rd of March

Mum just stayed in bed most of the day yesterday. And I didn't even want to talk to her. So I just ate some of the roast and I hardly saw her till she came in my room to wake me up this morning. And the radio's on in the kitchen. And she's all dressed for going to work and saying she's in a rush. She's got to get there early because of the stock-taking thing this week. Then she tells me to make my own cup of tea because she's not going to have time and also to make sure I wear my new trainers.

And I'm thinking after all that happened at the weekend is WHAT TRAINERS I WEAR all she cares about?

And you could hear outside it was raining again. And I didn't feel like getting up or putting on any trainers or getting the minibus or anything. I just

pulled up the covers over me and decided if Mum's
going then I'm just going to miss the minibus and
stay put. Then I wouldn't have to put up with the
rain and the crap that goes on at school.

But Mum comes back in her coat and she
pulls the covers off and says I've got to get the
minibus. And I tell her to EFF OFF AND LEAVE
ME ALONE. And she says don't talk to her like
that. But I say I'll talk to her how I like. And she
says she knows I didn't like what happened at the
weekend. But I don't have to worry about it or
anything because she swears she's not going to
start TAKING HEROIN AGAIN.

And she's saying all she did was take some of it to
relax a bit. Then she says, "Jon's the same. He only
takes it to relax now and then. And he's not selling
it like he was. Because he doesn't want to mess up
people's lives."

Then she doesn't say anything for a bit and neither

do I. Then she says she's got to go and I've got to
get up. But I don't. And she goes anyway because
she's got to.

And I lie back. And I'm thinking WHAT HAPPENS
IF I STAY THERE AND DON'T GO? And one
thing is I don't want to miss the next bit in THE
FIREBIRD story. Then everyone else would hear
it except me. And in the end I get up and get
dressed.

And I don't bother with any tea or anything.
I just sit there with music on the radio until I hear
Keith honk the horn. Then I go down. And it's all
grey out like there's no sky today. And I try to stop
getting wet by putting my bag on my head.

And everyone's pretty quiet on the minibus. And
that's all right because they're mainly a bunch of
DOPEHEADS who I don't even want to talk to.
So I look out the window. And Keith drives away.

And there's a woman going past the shops with a boy who must be in about Year One. And she's trying to pull him to keep him under her umbrella. And I remember Mum said to me a few weeks ago she thinks I'll be a GOOD DAD ONE DAY. But I don't want to be some crazy kid's Dad. And the Mum and the boy are going faster than us because it takes ages to get past the roundabout because of the traffic. But we get to Heronford in the end.

And Raju's still away. And Nathan's got a split lip from something that's happened at the weekend. Then at breakfast Pete is KING OF THE CRAP JOKES as usual because he says we're starting the week with KNOCK-KNOCK JOKES. And Shabana says she doesn't understand what's meant to be funny about KNOCK-KNOCK JOKES. Then Pete says he bets he can make her laugh. And he starts telling KNOCK-KNOCK JOKES. And it's like he's got a whole book of them in his head.

KNOCK KNOCK.
WHO'S THERE?
HOWARD.
HOWARD WHO?
HOWARD I KNOW?
And then

KNOCK KNOCK.
WHO'S THERE?
NANA.
NANA WHO?
NANA YOUR BUSINESS.

And they're all crap like that. And Shabana never even laughs. But some people are laughing more because of how she keeps saying to Pete, "WHAT'S MEANT TO BE FUNNY ABOUT THAT?"

And I'm sitting there feeling about the same as her to be honest.

Then something weird happens because Raymond's putting sugar in his tea but the spoon slips and the sugar spills on the table. Then straightaway Raymond just starts crying. And he's trying not to show it but he's crying so there are tears on his face. And Shabana tries to talk to him. But he doesn't say anything. He's just crying.

And usually everyone at school laughs if anyone cries. But no one laughed that time when Raymond was crying. And Pete took him out in the corridor. And Shabana went to the sink to get a cloth. And I wanted the Nutella which Barry's got. So I said, "Pass the Nutella Barry."

And he pretends he can't reach far enough. Then he says, "Sorry." And he makes out he's trying to push it closer but he can't. And some days I'd have PUNCHED HIS LIGHTS OUT for doing that.

But I felt too tired to even bother. So all I did was look at him like he's BRAIN-DEAD. And he says, "Come on then! You don't frighten me! Nothing frightens me!" But Shabana comes back and asks, "What's your problem now Barry?"

And then he had to shut up.

And she wipes up Raymond's sugar and takes the cloth back to the sink.

Then Barry says to me, "Is your mum coming on Friday or have they locked her in the loony-bin again?"

And he thought he was being very clever. But in fact he said it just when Pete came back. And he didn't even notice Pete was behind him.

And Pete says, "I think that's VERY RUDE Barry." So then Barry's sitting there like A CONFUSED HAMSTER. And Pete looks at me. And I'm eating my toast with nothing on it. And he says, "Good ignoring Jason Dooley," like he always frigging says.

Anyway then we do Pete's dumb FEELINGS thing.
And I said I'm ALL RIGHT.

Then we're with Richard. And he's smiling away in
a green shirt like he's caught something from Pete.
And we do a WARM-UP GAME which is singing.
And then some other thing with clicking fingers
and stamping feet.
Then Richard gives out the instruments and I get
the xylophone again because he says he wants
me to be the one who plays the xylophone in the
performance. And I say I haven't even had a turn
on the DJEMBE yet. And he says he knows that
and I'm not the only one but we all will have a
turn.
Then he gives the djembe to Barry. So then Barry's
sitting there happy as a puppy because he's got
the djembe. And Richard says we're going to do
that thing we did on Friday with me playing the

xylophone. And it's the TRAVELLING TRAVELLING TRAVELLING song. Because he says he wants us to do it in the performance. And a few people start complaining that they don't like the instrument they've got. Then Pete stands up and he tells us all to SETTLE DOWN AND LISTEN TO RICHARD.

And Richard says it's me going to start the song by doing my tune on the xylophone. But I've only got one xylophone stick. So Richard finds another one. But when I get up to get it Barry Holmes picks up the other stick and tries to play my tune on the xylophone even though he doesn't know how. And Shabana tells him to leave my xylophone alone.

Then I sit down again and Richard says for me to play the tune.

But I try and it's wrong because I can't remember where it starts on the xylophone. And Barry and some of the others think that's VERY FUNNY.

Then Richard shows me the place and gets this red felt-tip and says I can mark on the xylophone where I've got to start.

So I do it.

Then I'm giving the pen back to Richard and Barry starts trying to play my tune again. And this time I just swing round and stick the felt tip right in his fat arm. And he swings back so quickly that the xylophone stick hits Nazrul in the face or something because Nazrul shouts out. And Shabana holds me to stop anything getting worse. But it's too late because Nazrul's got Barry by his throat. And Barry's trying to push him off. And Pete pulls Nazrul away. But even so Barry punches him in his face. And then Nazrul punches Barry back and spits at him and he shouts in Bengali and then he kicks the djembe so hard it hits into the wall and makes a dent in it.

And Shabana lets go of me because I'm not doing

anything. And she tries to get Barry.

And Richard's sitting there holding the cowbell like if anyone goes near him he's going to whack them with it.

And Pete's holding Nazrul. And Shabana gets Barry so he's lying on the floor. And then I don't know why but Raymond just flips too. So now it's like TAG WRESTLING or something. Because Raymond starts going RIPE BANANAS. And the pencil-pots and line-guides go flying.

And Pete's trying to hold Nazrul with one arm and get Raymond with the other.

And Barry's kicking and shouting out that Shabana's hurting him.

And Pete's saying to Raymond, "I'M JUST GOING TO STOP YOU HURTING YOURSELF OR ANYONE ELSE!"

And Nazrul's acting like his TROUSERS ARE ON FIRE. And he shakes himself away from Pete. Then

he kicks over some chairs and shouts more stuff
in Bengali and storms out and sets off the fire
alarm when he goes out.

So this fire alarm noise starts very loud because
they turn it up loud so we don't like setting it off.
And Liam comes in and he's helping with Raymond
who's shouting he's got to get his asthma inhaler.
And Wendy's got Nazrul out in the corridor. Then
she opens the door and tells us the fire alarm's
going AS IF WE CAN'T FRIGGING HEAR IT.
Though no one's actually lining up. And Pete says
"I CAN'T BELIEVE THIS. WHAT DOES IT MEAN
WHEN A FIRE ALARM GOES OFF?" And Nathan
tells him, "In our house it means my mum's cooking
chicken."
But we've got to go out and line up in the
playground. So we go out there in the rain with
the other classes. And no one's fighting any more

but we're all looking about in case it starts up.
And Pete's scratching the scar on his neck. And
Nazrul's at the back being quiet but looking like
he's bubbling inside like a pan full of chips. And
Richard's there in his green shirt and he's still
holding the COWBELL.

And Wendy gets the fire alarm turned off. Then we
can go back in.

And Pete says NO PUSHING. But Barry does push
so Nazrul kicks him. And Pete says they've both
lost their bonuses.

And Nazrul looks like he couldn't care. But Barry's
complaining it wasn't him. And he tells Nazrul to
watch out BECAUSE HE KNOWS ALL THE KUNG
FU PRESSURE POINTS YOU CAN KILL SOMEONE
WITH which sounds like pure crap to my ears.

Then we're back in the classroom except Nazrul's
got to go with Shabana to say sorry to Richard for
kicking the djembe. And also Raymond stays with

Liam. And Pete wants total quiet. And Wendy's in there picking the things off the floor.

And Pete says we're going to miss the rest of the lesson with Richard because our BEHAVIOUR'S TERRIBLE AND IT'S NEARLY BREAK ANYWAY. And he tells us all to sit up straight with our feet on the floor. But no one's listening properly so he shouts out, "I HAVEN'T GOT YOUR ATTENTION."

And Wendy comes across and stands with her arms folded and looking down her nose at us and says, "LISTEN TO PETE!" Then she asks, "WHO'S FEELING PROUD OF THEIR BEHAVIOUR?"

But no one says anything back about that.

And Pete says it looks like we won't even be doing Aaron's lesson. And I don't say anything but Barry and Paolo say they want to hear the story. Then Pete says we won't unless WE STOP ACTING LIKE A BUNCH OF KIDS HALF OUR AGE.

And Nazrul comes back with Shabana. And he

looks like he's trying to give Barry THE EVIL EYE when he sits down.

And Pete asks, "How did all this start?"

And he's looking at Barry. And Barry says, "Jason STABBED me."

And I say, "I DIDN'T!"

But Barry holds out his arm and says, "Look!"

And everyone's looking at his fat arm. And he says, "There's a red mark and everything."

And I say, "That's because it was a RED PEN!"

And Wendy says, "So you DID stab him!"

And I say, "I didn't STAB him! It was a FELT TIP!"

But before I can say anything more Wendy goes, "They're not going to take you at HALIMER unless you learn to SHOW SOME SELF CONTROL!"

And I say, "Why is everyone always STARTING ON ME?"

And I get up and grab the nearest thing which is the tray of Pritt sticks and I chuck it at Barry.

But it misses him and hits Wendy. Then Pete and her grab at me. And Nazrul kicks the tray so that it whacks into Barry's legs. And Barry starts swearing. And I don't know what happened after that because Wendy's taking me in the corridor and saying to me if I don't stop there was going to be trouble. BUT THERE WAS ALREADY TROUBLE WASN'T THERE?

Then Nazrul and Barry have got to sit out there with me. And Wendy's telling us TAKE DEEP BREATHS and COUNT UP TO TEN which she always says even though it doesn't frigging work.

And we have to sit there being silent. And I don't even look at Barry or Nazrul. I just stare at a map of the world that's on the wall.

And it's wet break so no one goes out anyway. But we still have to stay in the corridor.

And Liam comes down so he's with us instead of Wendy. And he stands there and says something like, "Remember EVEN IF YOU'RE IN A BIG HOLE at least you're not BURIED UNDER THE EARTH AS WELL." Which is the sort of crap Liam always says and the only one who thinks it's clever is him.

Then Pete goes past and says to Liam he's calling off the lesson with Aaron.

And I wish I'd stayed in bed in the end because the main thing that made me come to school was hearing what's going to happen in the FIREBIRD STORY.

And I'm thinking some memories about when they put me in that home when things were bad with Mum. And when I was there I spent most of the time either getting into fights that I didn't even want to happen or watching children's TV because it was how to forget about the place you were.

And the people who worked there said I had
BEHAVIOUR DIFFICULTIES. Though if you ask
me they had behaviour difficulties themselves. But
at least me being there made Mum sort herself
out because that was when she went to this place
called THE TWO STORIES CENTRE which is where
you go when you want to stop taking drugs. And
that's called REHAB.

And I knew she was there but I wasn't allowed to
go and see her.

And I was hoping she was managing it and
she was getting better and I could go home and
be normal.

And she was there all the summer. And all I ever
heard from her was a birthday card.

Then she came out which meant she wasn't
taking drugs. And she started doing her BACK-
TO-WORK COURSE and then got her job in the

shoe shop which is what she still does now. And
my Educational Welfare Officer Marie went to
see her. And she said because Mum wasn't taking
drugs it was all right if I went home.
And that was the best news of my life because
I wasn't going to be in a home where you're locked
in and people write down stuff about you the
whole time.
And I know Mum was happy I came back
because she got a new TV with the best channels.
And when I got home and saw it she didn't say
anything. She just watched when I was working
out how to use the remote control. And she stood
there and looked happy about it.

And I'm sitting there remembering that. Then
Aaron shows up and he asks Pete if he's all right.
And Pete looks back and says, "I think I can feel a
stress-related illness coming on."

Then he says sorry to Aaron but it's been a bad morning and there's only Micah and Nathan in the classroom. So it's probably not worth Aaron doing the lesson.

But Aaron says he'll try. And he goes in and you can hear him trying to do a lesson. And after a bit they're laughing at something. And Pete says if me, Nazrul and Barry are ON OUR BEST BEHAVIOUR then he'll let us back in. And we all say yes. So he lets us go.

And everyone's sitting on the comfortable chairs and Aaron's starting a story that's about Nasruddin.

He says one day there's a robber who comes in Nasruddin's house and he takes everything he can carry. So that's all Nasruddin's best clothes and silver cups and his cushions and everything. But then just when he's leaving with Nasruddin's things Nasruddin comes back and he sees the robber's taking his things. But he doesn't say anything or shout out about the robber or anything. He just follows him. And the robber goes right across the town. And Nasruddin follows him. And the robber gets to his house. And Nasruddin follows him in. And when the robber's putting down the stuff he took Nasruddin gets in the bed. And then the robber sees him. And he says to Nasruddin, "What are you doing?"

And Nasruddin says, "My wife and family will be along soon."

And the robber says, "What do you mean?"

And Nasruddin says, "WELL WE ARE MOVING TO YOUR HOUSE AREN'T WE?"

And then you should see how Shabana was laughing because of the story. And everyone looks at her and is laughing too. And Pete was smiling a bit at last.

Then Aaron starts saying how the performance is coming now because it's already Monday and the performance is on Friday. And he shows us he's got some of our poems that he typed. And he gives them to us. And he says how he likes them.

Then he says in the performance he wants Nathan and Paolo to read out their FIREBIRD FEATHER POEMS. And Nathan says all right. But Paolo isn't very sure about it because he says he can't even read properly. But Aaron says he can learn the poem BY HEART because it's only three lines long. So Paolo says he'll try.

Then Aaron says I'm going to read out my horse poem in the performance and Micah can too because his horse poem is good. And Micah says he will. And I say I'll try.

Then Aaron asks, "Do we want to go back to the FIREBIRD story?"

And everyone does. So he asks what was the last

bit we heard? And Paolo says it's the hunter boy having to go and get the wedding dress out of the sea. And Aaron says THAT'S RIGHT.

Then he says the thing where he goes, "THERE ARE FOUR DIRECTIONS. NORTH SOUTH EAST AND WEST. BUT WE ARE GOING IN THE FIFTH DIRECTION WHICH IS THE DIRECTION OF STORIES."

And after that he starts the next bit of the story. And it starts with the boy standing there with the King. And the King tells him to go and get the wedding dress or he'll cut his head off. And the boy doesn't like that. So he walks out of the King's room feeling angry because there's nothing but trouble for him since he picked up the feather. But his horse is there and like usual it says, "What did I tell you about being in trouble and finding

out the meaning of pain? But don't worry about it.
Jump on me and let's go."

And so they went across the 27 countries until
they got to The Land of Never again. Then the
boy stops the horse and gets off. And there's the
sea and the water going away until it looks as if it
goes away for ever.

And the boy's thinking HOW CAN I EVER FIND
A DRESS IN ALL THAT SEA?

And then there's a sound of a voice that says,
"HELP ME! HELP ME!"

And it's a crab because the horse has trodden on
it so the crab can't move. And the crab is saying
"HELP! HELP!"

So the hunter boy says to the horse, "Let it go!"

And the crab's happy. It says, "Thank you for saving
my life because I was stuck there. And you don't
know something about me but I'M THE KING OF
THE CRABS. And can I do something to help you?"

And the boy said, "Yes you can. The Princess has got a wedding dress but it's under a stone under the sea. And I've got to get it."

Then the crab did a sort of whistle and the water in the sea started moving. Then slowly out came all these crabs. Like hundreds of them or thousands. And the KING OF THE CRABS said they had to go and find the dress. And they went in the sea and it took them one hour. Then they brought the dress. So then the boy thanks the crabs and gets the dress and then the horse rides him back across the countries to the palace. And he goes to find the King with the dress.

Then Aaron says that's all of the story he's going to tell this year. And when he COMES BACK NEXT YEAR he's going to say what happens at the end. And everyone says next year's too long. And Aaron's smiling away like he thinks it's the

funniest joke anyone ever made. And Shabana asks
him when he's really going to tell the end because
she doesn't want to miss it. And Aaron says he'll
tell us it but not tomorrow because there's still a
lot to happen in the story. Then he says it's time to
do some writing. And he says we're going to do a
group poem instead of poems on our own. Then he
asks what the hunter's feeling when the King said to
go and get the dress from the sea.
And Micah says ANGRY.
And Aaron nods and says so we can write a group
poem about what it feels like when you get angry.
And Aaron says what colour is it when you're angry.
And Nathan says RED AND ORANGE. So
Aaron puts that.
And then he says what temperature is it like?
And I say BOILING.
And then he says what's the sound of being
angry like?

And Barry says THUNDER.

And then he says what smell is it like?

And he gets Nazrul to say something. And Nazrul says it's like the smell of A VOLCANO.

And Aaron's writing all that down and some other ideas about A DRILL and CHINESE FIGHTING FISH and THE SEA.

Then we have to do the same about what it feels like when you've calmed down. And we gave ideas and then he reads out the poem. And that's the end.

Then next thing it's dinner. And then the ones who've got mainstream on Monday go off. Except Nazrul stays because of what happened.

And I've been writing this.

And Pete's says he's ordered a GYPSY BAND to play for us at breakfast tomorrow to get us in a better mood than we were today.

But the only one who still seems to be in a bad

mood now is Barry because he still thinks he's going to have a fight with Nazrul. And he said he's going to MASH NAZRUL'S HEAD SO IT LOOKS LIKE A MASHED POTATO. But if I was Nazrul I wouldn't worry very much. Because I'd be more frightened of a DUSTPAN AND BRUSH than of Barry Holmes.

Tuesday 24th

Mum had to go the shop early again because of
that STOCK-TAKING. And it was like yesterday
because she woke me up but straightaway she was
saying she was late and she had to go.
But I got up and got the minibus and everything.
And when we got there Raju was back. And Nazrul
had to see Liam to talk about what happened
yesterday.
Then at breakfast Pete says we've all got to pick
our TOP THREE BREAKFAST CEREALS OF ALL
TIME but it couldn't be COCOPOPS because
they turn the milk brown. And Pete's all right
as a teacher. And there are things he's good at.
Like you can trust him because if you give him
swimming money to look after and then you don't
go swimming and you forget about him having
your money he'll still give it back. But when he

gets ideas like WHAT ARE YOUR TOP THREE
BREAKFAST CEREALS OF ALL TIME BUT IT
CAN'T BE COCOPOPS BECAUSE THEY TURN
THE MILK BROWN you wish you could just zip up
his mouth and have breakfast in a bit of peace
and quiet.

Anyway then it was time for FEELINGS. And when
it was my turn I got up and I decided I wasn't just
going to pick ALL RIGHT straightaway. Instead I
spent a long time looking at the different feelings
you can choose. And you could see that Pete's
hopes were getting up because it looked as if I was
going to say I was WORRIED or something like
that. And I kept looking as if I was going to do
that.
But then I picked ALL RIGHT just to annoy Pete.
And I sat back down.
And Pete didn't say anything. He just went

on to Micah who always takes it seriously and says something like he's feeling a mixture of DISAPPOINTED, EXCITED and DEPRESSED.

Then Aaron came in. And today he started with riddles because he said he was checking to see if we're awake yet.

And what he said was
WHAT GETS HARDER TO CATCH WHEN YOU RUN?

And no one knew that. And Aaron said if Liam was there he was going to say A RABBIT. Then he gave us some clues. And then Shabana got the answer which is YOUR BREATH.

Then Aaron asked
WHY IS CINDERELLA RUBBISH AT FOOTBALL?

And the answer is

BECAUSE HER COACH IS A PUMPKIN.

Then he reads the poem about BEING ANGRY
that we did yesterday. And he asked if it was any
good. And most of us said it was all right. But
he was looking interested in it like Micah does
when he's choosing what he's feeling. And he said
Richard's going to work on it with us so we could
do some ANGRY MUSIC to go with it.
And that shouldn't be too difficult for us lot.
Then Aaron says if we're going to read out a poem
in the performance then we've got to practise it
every day now because it's only 3 days till
the performance.
So Nathan had to read out first. And Aaron got
him to stand up. And he said the rest of us had
to listen properly then say WHAT WAS GOOD and
WHAT COULD BE BETTER about how he did it.

So we did that.

And Paolo tried his firebird feather poem but the only comment was he hadn't learnt it properly.

Then I had to do my faithful horse poem. And I felt pretty DUMB doing it. And Aaron asked what comments people wanted to say. And Raju had to be a CLEVER LITTLE CREEP AS USUAL because he said the problem with the way I read it was I WAS SCRATCHING MY HEAD LIKE I'VE GOT NITS.

Then everyone was laughing their heads off about that. And I could have said something back to show what a little DIPSTICK Raju is. But I didn't bother.

And Pete looked angry and said Raju's comment was COMPLETELY INAPPROPRIATE. Then he said what I did was GOOD IGNORING which he loves saying so much he says it about forty times every day.

Then he got Raymond to say a sensible comment
which was MY VOICE WAS TOO QUIET.
Then Aaron got me to do it again. And
straightaway Pete said my voice was better and
louder. But then even though my head wasn't even
itching I couldn't help scratching it. And when
I did it Raju pulled this face like he was saying
WHAT DID I TELL YOU?
Then everyone was laughing all over again because
he was dissing me.
But I just sat down when I finished and Aaron
said for people to be quiet because what I did
was good.
Then Micah did his horse poem which was all right.

Then after that Aaron said, "DO YOU WANT
TO HEAR THE NEXT BIT OF THE STORY?" And
everyone says yes except Raju says NO.
And Aaron says to him then why doesn't he go out

and stand in the rain instead?

And everyone's laughing at that because it's Raju getting dissed by Aaron. And Raju shuts his mouth at last.

Then Aaron says, "Where are we in the story?"

And the last bit was the hunter boy taking the dress into the palace to give it to the King.

Then Aaron says the King looks happy when the boy gets there with the dress because it means he can get married to the Princess now. And he gives the hunter boy more coins. And also he makes him like the most important sort of person you could be which is a LORD or something.

Then straightaway he says to the Princess, "All right. Here's the dress. So now you've got to marry me."

But the Princess didn't. She shook her head and said, "I'm only going to marry you after this hunter boy gets put in a BIG POT FULL OF BOILING WATER."

Then you can imagine what happens because straightaway the King says to the soldiers that are there, "All right then. Go and get a big pot full of water and boil it and then put the hunter in it."

And then the hunter is the saddest he's been in all the story because he's going to be put in a pot full of boiling water. And that means you'll be burnt to death in a few slow moments.

And the soldiers get the pot. And they put water in.

And they make a fire under the big metal pot.

And it starts to heat up.

And the boy's looking in because the water slowly starts steaming.

And all he can think of is he has to say goodbye to his horse before it happens. So he asks the King to let him see his horse quickly.

And the King says, "Go and see your horse."

Then Aaron said that was all of the story he was

going to say today. And he asked what we thought was going to happen. But he said all our ideas were wrong. And he said tomorrow we'll find out because he was going to tell the last bit of the story.

Then there were ten minutes left. And he got us all to write a poem where we described what looking at the hot water would be like if we were the boy. And what the boy was feeling then. And he said that it was going to be the beginning of the poem. And tomorrow we're going to get to the end of the story and also finish writing the poem.

Then it was break. And we saw Richard after and we did the fast drumming which is my favourite out of what we do with Richard. And I GOT TO PLAY THE DJEMBE at last. And Richard said to try to remember the drumming solo I was meant to do in the performance last year and play it in the middle of the fast drumming. And I did it. And

Barry was on the tambourine and Richard said for him to do a solo on the tambourine too and he nearly wasn't going to do it. Then Pete put on an AMERICAN VOICE and said, "SOCK IT TO ME BARRY!"

And that made Barry laugh and he ended up doing it. Then the rest of the lesson was normal.

And in the afternoon I've been writing this down. But now it's almost time to go home. So Pete says when I've finished writing I've got to help him put things away.

Wednesday

I'm in the kitchen at home now and the floor's got smashed up plates all over. And it's just me here in the flat. But it's still an hour till the minibus is coming. So I'm going to write down about what happened.

Yesterday at school was all right. But then when I got home I'm just going in the door when someone shoves me and comes in. And it's Jon. And he shuts the door quick and he's out of breath and wearing this white baseball cap. And he says, "Jacey boy. I need a favour."

Then he reaches in his pocket. And he gets out this packet. And it's a taped-up plastic bag the same as I got for him from his GIRAFFE FRIEND. And he says to me, "Keep this and hide it and don't tell anyone. And I'll be back to get it."

And I just look at it.

And Jon says, "I'VE GOT PEOPLE AFTER ME AND I'M NOT WAITING!"

Then he grabs my hand and shoves the packet in it. And he says, "TAKE IT AND HIDE IT!"

And he's acting like I'm still going to do anything he says like when I was a kid. But I don't want to. And even though my voice comes out sort of funny I say, "I don't want it."

And I give the packet back in his hand but it falls on the floor.

Then it's like a dog bit Jon or something because he rams me up against the wall and he's got his plaster cast pushing in my throat so it's strangling me. And he says, "DO WHAT I TELL YOU JACEY BOY! BECAUSE WHEN I GET ANGRY YOU KNOW WHAT HAPPENS!"

Then he pushes me on the floor next to the packet and tells me, "PICK IT UP!"

But I won't touch it.

And Jon gets on the floor and his teeth are showing. And he butts his head right next to mine and says, "DO WHAT I TELL YOU OR I'M GOING TO HURT YOU WORSE THAN I EVER DID!"

And he says, "I MEAN IT JACEY! I'LL HURT YOU SO MUCH IT'LL TAKE YOU MORE THAN A LIFETIME TO FORGET IT!"

And I pick the packet up then.

And Jon gets up. But I don't.

And he says, "Hide it. And not a squeak to your mother."

Then he opens the door like he's going. But he looks round and says, "You still want to join the army?"

And I start getting up. But I'm feeling too sick to say anything back to him.

And he stands there and says it again. "You still want to join the army Jacey boy?"

And he's looking calmer now. And I shake my
head.
Then he says, "Good thing because they wouldn't
have a wimp like you!"
And he steps out and pulls his baseball cap down.
And the door bangs shut. And he's gone.
And I'm not doing what he says.
I don't want to do what he says EVER AGAIN.
And I don't know what he's GOING TO DO IF
I DON'T.
Maybe he'll kill me.
But I'm thinking I'D RATHER BE DEAD
ANYWAY.
And I sit back on the floor.
And questions are buzzing round me like wasps.
I think what happens if someone who's after him
saw him come up here and next thing they're
kicking in the door to get the packet? And now
it's here what am I going to do with it if I don't

hide it? What happens if I give it to Mum? Or the police? Or I take it to school and give it to Pete?"

But one thing for sure is I'm not just sitting there like that. So I get my bike and put Jon's packet in my pocket and I think I'm going to the shop and I'm going to tell Mum about what's happening. And when I'm going down the steps with my bike I feel sure about it. And even though it's raining again I just head up the road in the rain.

Then I see a man in this white cap walking quickly past the shops. And I think it's Jon. So I slow down. But when I'm closer I see it's not anyone even like him. So I keep going. But even so I'm thinking about what he said about what he's going to do if I say something to Mum. Because he said he's going to HURT ME WORSE THAN BEFORE. And he's hurt me a lot before. And he told me never to tell a word to anyone about what he did. And I didn't. I didn't want anyone to know anyway. But as I was cycling I was remembering about it. And I'm going to write it because then it explains what I did with the packet.

It happened ages back when Jon was still going out with Mum. But it was after that time when the man didn't pay and Jon started hitting me. And since that happened I never liked doing things for him any more. And him and Mum were arguing pretty much non-stop. And I was sick of it. But I couldn't stop him coming in the flat and neither could Mum. He had the keys and he used to just come in. And Mum kept saying he wasn't coming back any more. But he always did.
Then he showed up near to Christmas one morning. And it was the sort of cold day that means you don't want to go out. But Mum was at the doctor

because she had a cough that wouldn't stop. And she was at the doctor to see if he could give her something for it. And Jon just comes in the front door. And then he makes a fried-egg sandwich. Then he puts on the telly and he sits there eating his fried-egg sandwich and watching MTV on the telly. And then he says HE NEEDS ME TO DO HIM A FAVOUR.

And I told him, "I don't want to."

And it was the first time I ever said I wasn't going.

And I remember Jon eats a bit and then he says, "Well here's a newsflash for you Jacey. You're going."

And I said it was cold. And he says something like, "You'll be colder without your mum."

And I didn't know what that meant.

Then he said, "Without me your mum'll sink faster than the effing Titanic."

And I didn't like how he said that. So what I

remember is I told him, "Eff off!" And I said, "I'm not going."

And I tried just walking in the kitchen because normally he didn't bother even getting off the sofa.

But this time he got up so fast it surprised me. And he grabbed my wrist and twisted me so his face was right up near mine and says, "Don't you EVER talk to me like that!"

And I tried to pull my arm away but he holds on to it so strongly you could feel you couldn't get away by pulling. So I kicked him. And it got him right in the knee and it probably hurt because he sort of backed away. But he didn't let go. Then I swung an elbow to try and hit his face and got him sort of half on the cheek and half on the nose. But it didn't make him leave off. He twisted my arm round more than I've ever felt before. And it hurt so much I thought my elbow was breaking or

something and I dropped down. But he gripped on
to my head with his fingers and that kept me up on
my feet. And he didn't say anything all that time.

But then he did the worst thing anyone ever did
to me. He turned on the gas. On the cooker. He
turned it on and clicked it so the gas came on.
And I couldn't understand. I thought he must be
going to start cooking. But he still had one hand
gripping my wrist. And he yanked my hand on top
of the flame. It was the underneath of my hand
near my wrist. It was right above where the gas
was and I shouted because it hurt so much. And
he took it away. But he didn't let go.
And he was sweating I remember. But the look on
his face was this nothing look. And he said,
"You going to do what I tell you?"
And I couldn't even make my voice work because
I was just trying to breathe because of what he

did. But when I didn't say anything he moved my hand back close on top of the flame.

That's what Jon did.

And even though I tried to push myself back by kicking against the oven as hard as I could he didn't budge. And it was burning the skin that was already burnt. And while he was doing it there was this happy music singing out from the telly. And I was shouting and kicking. But Jon was like a stone you can't budge. He held my hand there and nothing would stop him except when I said, "I'll do it."

Then straightaway he said, "Good boy." And he let's go. And then I'm crying because I was still just a kid.

And he says, "Put some water on it."

And he helps me. And he looks at my hand and says it'll be all right.

And I stopped crying even though it hurt.

And Jon got an envelope and said to take it to this man down in the betting shop and bring back the money.

And then he said, "And keep quiet about what just happened. BECAUSE IF YOU EVER SAY A WORD ABOUT IT TO ANYONE I SWEAR I'LL MAKE YOU AND YOUR MOTHER WISH YOU WERE DEAD!"

And I remember exactly how he said that. He said it twice.

"I'LL MAKE YOU AND YOUR MOTHER WISH YOU WERE DEAD!"

And I took the envelope to the betting shop.

And Mum saw what my hand was like later and I said to her I spilt the kettle on it. And that thing about the kettle was all I ever said to anyone about what Jon did until I wrote this down now.

And round then was the time when I got in

my worst trouble at my old school which was MOORCROFT. And I got kicked out mainly because I threw a fire extinguisher at the Head Teacher. But that wasn't the only thing. And so I ended up at Heronford instead.

And all of that memory was going on in my head as I was going up towards the roundabout. And it makes me think DON'T TELL MUM. So instead of turning down the road where the shop is I turn the other way. And I go round the back of the shops to the river.

And I head along towards the ramp. And there's nobody about. I ride along and there's just rain splashing in the river.

And I know if I do tell Mum then it means there's going to be trouble for sure. Because she'll probably go crazy about it when she finds out I've been helping Jon sell drugs and never told her.

And maybe she'll go to the police another time.

And Jon's going to know it was me who told Mum

after he said DON'T TELL HER. And then what's

he going to do?

And I'm riding and thinking why do I have to tell

her?

I can keep the packet and hide it.

And if people are after Jon maybe he won't even

come back.

And if he does come I can just give it to him like

he said.

Then that might be the end of it.

And I can feel the hard corner of the packet.

It's digging in my leg every time I pedal round.

And I reach down to move it.

Then I don't even think but I chuck it in the river.

And it splashes in there with the rain and goes

a bit under.

Then it comes up and it's floating in the river.

And that's what I did.

Jon's packet's out there in the river going away with the water and the rain.

And Mum wasn't back yet when I got in. I took my top off but just sat there still with wet trousers.

And I put on Sky Sports News and sat watching.

But I wasn't concentrating on it because of what I just did.

And part of me felt like I just did the best thing ever.

And part of me felt like it was completely the dumbest thing.

And Mum got in after a bit and starts going on about me about watching TV in wet trousers and says to put on something dry.

And I get changed and there's food she's cooked.

And we're eating and I try to say something about Jon. But I CAN'T SAY IT. It's like Jon's eyes are still there looking.

And there's Champion's League on. And I want to watch it. And I think AFTER THE GAME I'LL SEE ABOUT TELLING MUM.

But in the second half she said she was tired. So she had a bath. Then she went to bed before the game was even over.

And I stayed sitting there and not going to bed for ages. Different programmes started and finished on the telly but I was sitting there with it all in my head.

And when I did go to bed I kept waking up. Because how am I meant to know what's going to happen now?

And I felt as though I stayed awake nearly all night. But I must have gone to sleep for a bit because next thing I heard was the kettle and the radio and Mum getting ready for work.

Then she came in and said she was going in a few minutes.

So I went in the kitchen. And she made me some tea. Then they said the time on the radio. And it wasn't even seven. And Mum said she was up earlier because she was meant to be getting to the shop at 7.30 this week but every day so far she got there late. And she finished her tea and said she had to go. And she said she wouldn't be back till 6 because there was still a lot to do for the stock-taking. And I never said anything about last night. Then when she's putting on her coat she asks me about how the thing at school is going with the music. And I tell her it's all right.

And she says, "I know you've got this performance. But I don't know when we'll get the stock-taking done. And if we're still doing it on Friday then I don't know if I'll be able to make it."

And she picks up her bag. And something in me is like a storm starting. Because I shoved the cup of tea she made me off the table so it went on the floor. And I say, "YOU NEVER COME!"

Then I shoved the whole tray of washing up on the floor and it smashed some big plates that were a present from my Grandad when he was alive.

And Mum was saying, "Stop it Jason. Stop it. Stop it Jason."

And she was almost crying. But she didn't touch me.

And I got her tea cup that was finished and threw it against the wall.

And she just kept saying, "STOP IT!"

And I remember what her voice sounded like because it wasn't angry. It sounded tired. Because it was like she knew I wasn't going to stop however many times she said for me to stop.

And some of what I threw was just pans that

just hit the wall and banged on the floor. But the plates smashed.

And Mum didn't pick anything up or say anything more. She just left me here and went to work.

Then I stood in the smashed stuff. And they said the time again on the radio. And it was still only a bit after seven. So I got my journal book and then I'm writing this. But Keith's honking outside. So I'm going.

Wednesday at night.

It's late and Mum's asleep now but after what today was like I'm not tired or anything. So I'm writing some more now.

The morning was normal. It's Raymond's birthday. And we were all in except Nazrul. And Raymond brought a bottle of Fanta which you can do when it's your birthday and also these little cakes which I didn't want because they looked like they were for old ladies or something. But Barry Holmes didn't mind about that because he must have stuffed about three of them in his gob at breakfast.

And Raymond was looking pretty happy because he was telling Pete he got a football game from his foster parents.

And Pete's tucking into the cakes himself.

And he comes up with this thing that he wants
to know what we're going to do when we grow up.
And Raymond's got to say it first because it's his
birthday. Then Raymond says he's going to be A
FOOTBALLER which is a joke because Raymond's
so crap at football no team would have him except
perhaps CREWE ALEXANDRA. Then Raju says
what he's going to be is A STUNTMAN. And Barry
says what he's going to be is TALL ENOUGH TO
DUNK A BASKETBALL BACKWARDS. And Micah
says something I can't remember. And Pete asks
me. And I say I DON'T EVEN KNOW IF I WANT
TO GROW UP OR NOT. And Pete says FAIR
ENOUGH and keeps asking the others.
Then when we're going to Richard which is the
first lesson Pete says, "Are you feeling ill Jason?"
But I shake my head and tell him, "Just tired."
And he asks, "Didn't sleep much last night?"
And I shake my head.

Then we're with Richard and he's acting stressed-out because of the performance even though it's only Wednesday. And he makes us practise all the different things we've done like the TRAVELLING TRAVELLING TRAVELLING song and the FAST DRUMMING. And he also gets us to make up some new drumming to go with that ANGRY POEM we did with Aaron. And he said it was VERY GOOD when we played that. And at the end he was looking more chilled out and pleased. And he said tomorrow we're going to work with him and Aaron together in the hall because it's going to be called a DRESS REHEARSAL FOR THE PERFORMANCE.

Then it was break at last. So then we could play football. And after that it was Aaron. And everyone was asking

IS IT GOING TO BE THE END OF THE STORY?

And he said YES IT IS.

But first he started reading us some more poems he knows. And after that we had to practise our poem reading for the performance.

So Nathan does his FIREBIRD FEATHER POEM and that's all right.

And Paolo tries his one but he still hasn't learnt it because he kept stopping and asking Aaron what to say.

And then it was me meant to do my FAITHFUL HORSE POEM. But I said I wasn't doing it. And Aaron was trying to get me to do it and so was Shabana. But I wasn't going to. Then Pete said to Aaron to leave it for today because I was tired. So Aaron left it. And just Micah did his HORSE POEM.

Then it was time to hear what was going to be the end of the Firebird story. And Aaron said the last

thing was the hunter boy was going to get thrown
in a pot of boiling water. But he wanted to see his
horse first and so the King said, "Go and see your
horse."

So then the hunter boy walks out of the long
palace room and his horse is where it is the other
times.

And the boy says to the horse, "What's going to
happen now?" And he's almost crying. And he tells
the horse about going in the pot of boiling water.
And the horse says back, "I told you there was
going to be trouble and pain if you ever picked up
that feather. And now this is really it. But don't
worry because I know what you've got to do.
You've got to NOT HESITATE AND JUMP RIGHT
INTO THE BOILING WATER ON YOUR OWN."
So then the hunter boy went back. And the water
was bubbling and boiling because the pot was on
a fire.

And the King says to the soldiers, "RIGHT! PICK HIM UP AND THROW HIM IN THE BOILING WATER!"

But then the boy shakes his head and says, "DON'T TOUCH ME! BECAUSE I'M GOING TO JUMP IN ON MY OWN!"

He walks to the pot. And he does it. He jumps in.

And then it's a surprise what happens.

Because he starts getting out of the water.

And he's all right.

And in fact he looks as if he's changed. He's calm and stronger and looks better than he used to. And his eyes are strong.

And the King sees what's happened to the boy and he thinks, "If that's what that water does to you then I'm going to jump in there!"

And he goes up to it and then he jumps in the pot. But when he does it he gets BOILED TO DEATH STRAIGHTAWAY.

And then Aaron says, "Then they picked the hunter boy to be their new King. And it was him who was the one who got married to the Princess.

AND IF THEY DIDN'T LIVE
HAPPILY EVER AFTER THEN
THAT'S NOTHING TO DO
WITH YOU AND IT'S NOTHING
TO DO WITH ME."

Then that's the end of the story. And people clapped.

And Aaron said, "OK let's finish the poems we started doing yesterday about going in the hot water."

And this time we had to write about what it would be like to jump in the boiling water and then come out feeling different. So I wrote that and everyone did. And that was what we did with Aaron.

Then in the afternoon I was looking for this journal

to write something about what happened. But I remembered I left it back in the kitchen when I was in a hurry to get the minibus. So I'm writing all this back home now and it's late. But I'm going to try to write about everything else.

The afternoon at school was pretty much like normal. Pete got us to practise for the performance and then he was reading us a football story. Then I got the minibus home. But when I'm walking up to the flat I hear Jon's voice.

He says, "All right Jacey?"

And I can see he's there in the shadows where the lift is.

And for a moment I feel like ice or something. But I don't show it because I know how to stay looking normal.

And I say, "All right Jon?"

And he says, "I've come for my stuff."

And I've been thinking all day what to say if I see

him but now I don't say anything. All I'm thinking
is to try to get in the flat and shut the door. So I
start jogging up the stairs not as if I'm trying to
get away but just as if it's normal that I'm jogging
up the steps. And Jon's footsteps come after me.
And he says, "You kept it safe Jacey?"
And I'm already on our floor and running now.
And it feels like my hand's going to be shaking
trying to get the key in the door. And I don't want
Jon to see that. But actually it isn't shaking. The
key goes in. The door opens.
And Jon's saying another time, "You kept it safe?"
And I don't look round. I go in. I slam the door.
But it won't shut because Jon's foot's there.
And then I stop acting normal because I want
THE DOOR SHUT.
And Jon's going, "EH! Where's my stuff!"
But I don't say anything. I just shove at the door
with my new trainers pushing in the carpet and

my legs shoving and shoulders and arms pushing
and pushing. And it doesn't feel like Jon can push
properly because of how his arms are.

His feet slip. I can feel him slip.

And the door almost closes. The lock's nearly right
next to the bit it clicks into.

And I'm pushing so hard it twists my face.

And the lock's almost going to lock.

And even though Jon might be about to kill me
what's in my head is PETE AND HIS FRIGGING
RUGBY TRAINING. And I'm thinking if we'd done
some of that I could probably push the frigging
door shut.

And Jon says in a calm voice, "Let me in Jacey.
I need that stuff."

But the lock's almost clicking.

Then something changes.

You can feel from the door that Jon's moved and he's
got his shoulder or his back leaning on it. And he's

barging. And he says, "Stop it Jason! I'm coming in!"

And he shoves. And the door's opening.

And I dig my feet and try to push it back where it was nearly going to lock.

But it's opening. And it makes me growl a sound like a bear sound and BARGE BACK.

And maybe he wasn't expecting that because the door closes back.

And the lock clicks.

But it's a click because the lock on the door hits against the part on the wall. But it doesn't actually lock.

And Jon says, "You're getting strong Jacey boy! BUT NOT STRONG ENOUGH!"

And he really shoves. And he shoves again.

And there's nothing I can do then.

It's like he's a hammer and I'm a nail.

My trainers slip.

And I say, "GET OUT OF OUR FLAT!"

But his head's coming in.

And his face which is sweating.

And I'm ready for anything.

And he kicks the door so it slams shut behind him
and he says, "I'll get out when you give me my
stuff. Where is it?"

And he straightaway grabs the back of my head
and twists me so I'm walking in the living room.

And he's looking round.

But he can search the place all he frigging wants.

BECAUSE HE WON'T FIND THE STUFF.

And I say, "I haven't got it."

Then he shoves my head forward.

And he asks again and says, "DON'T MESS ABOUT!"

And I shout, "I CHUCKED IT IN THE RIVER!"

And he starts to laugh a bit down in his throat.

And he says, "You didn't."

And I say, "I THREW IT IN THE RIVER."

And he twists my head round and shoves his head

right against mine and shouts, "YOU DIDN'T. THAT STUFF'S WORTH TWO GRAND! NOT EVEN YOU'RE THICK ENOUGH TO CHUCK IT IN THE RIVER!"

And he cracks my head against the wall once and then another time harder.

And I tell him, "STOP IT!"

And he says, "Where is it?"

And I say "I THREW IT IN THE RIVER. BECAUSE I KNOW WHAT WAS IN IT! It's the heroin that messed up everything with Mum! And I DON'T WANT THAT AGAIN!"

And you could see that was the first time Jon properly believed me. And his face sort of went soft like he really wanted me to say, "Actually I've still got it."

But I don't say anything.

And he lets go of my head.

And his eyes are looking right at me.

And he seems white.

It's like he's frightened what he's going to do.

And he says, "You shouldn't mess with me Jason.

You shouldn't have done that!"

And I knew where I was going.

I go in the kitchen. I say, "COME ON!"

And he follows.

And I click on the gas.

And I look round and Jon stops where he is

because I put my hand on top of the flame.

And I say, "IS THIS WHAT YOU WANT TO

DO?"

And there's a smell of hairs burning on my arm.

And the flame's burning me.

But I do it and Jon can see it.

And I'm hardly feeling.

And I say, "COME ON!"

And that's what I kept saying, "COME ON!"

But Jon doesn't move. Every time I say it he just

stands still. And I see something I never thought would be true. Jon's scared. I know because I've seen boys at school like that. And I know they're scared.

And I say, "COME ON! HURT ME LIKE YOU DID WHEN I WAS A KID!"

And he says, "STOP IT!"

And he pulls me away from the cooker so hard I crash against a chair.

And then I can feel how much my hand's burnt.

And then there's the sound of the door. And Mum's voice.

She says, "JASON?"

And then she's rushing in the kitchen.

And she flashes.

I swear it's like a flash of light.

And she goes for Jon. She says, "Don't you lay a finger on him! I know what you did to him YOU BULLYING SCUMBAG!"

And I reckon if there was a knife there she'd have stabbed him.

But instead she's jabbing him in the chest so hard that Jon's going out in the living room. And she's shouting for him to get out or she'll RIP HIS FACE UP.

And she shoves him. Then he stops. And when he does she punches him.

And he shoves her back with his hand in her face. And I try to get him off her. Then he punches me on the side of my head so it knocks me over.

And you can see Mum's crying. But she's shouting, "I know about it! I know what you did! And it's not because he told me! He kept quiet! But he wrote about it! And I came back at lunchtime and his book thing was on the table! And it's all there what you did and how you kept him quiet!"

And I've got back up.

And Jon's touching his chin like he doesn't know

what to say now.

Then he says, "I gave him a packet worth two grand! And he chucked it in the river!"

And Mum says, "GOOD! THAT'S THE BEST EFFING PLACE FOR IT!"

Then she shoves him again. And she's shouting, "GET OUT OF HERE YOU PIG! YOU MAKE ME SICK! GET OUT OF HERE BEFORE I GET POLICE ROUND! GET OUT!"

And there doesn't seem to be any fight left in Jon.

He says, "Don't do this! You've got me wrong!"

But he's going down the hall now like a shopping trolley being pushed.

Then he's out the flat.

And the door slams.

And he shouts again, "You've got me wrong!"

Then he thumps the door once. Then the flat goes quiet.

And Mum just comes and drops on the sofa.
And there are tears all down her face. And she's
saying, "I don't want you taken off me again." And
she says, "WHAT HAVE I DONE JASON? WHAT
HAVE I DONE? WHAT HAVE I DONE?"
And it's all she says for a long time.
Then she gets calmer. And there's just a sound of
cars down in the street and the TV on next door.
And she sees how my hand's burnt. And she gets
some cream to put on it and this big plaster
to put on it. And it hurts but not like it hurt
last time.
And she asks me if I really threw Jon's stuff in the
river. And I tell her YES. And I say about all the
times Jon made me do things for him and what
he did if I said NO. And I tell her about that for
a long time. And even when it's things she knew
because of reading my journal book I still tell her
about it. And she keeps saying she's sorry because

it's her fault. But I tell her it's Jon's fault. And it's not
her fault. And she's the one who went to rehab and
stopped taking heroin. And then she's sitting there
crying and saying "You don't know how hard it was
to give it up."

And I tell her all I know is things got better since
she gave it up. And I tell her that since she went
to rehab she's been like the Mum I want. And she
looks like she can't believe what I'm saying. But
she doesn't say anything back. She just gets up. She
puts the kettle on. And I go in the kitchen with
her and she's making tea for us.

And she says she's sorry for reading my journal
book that's private but she came back at
lunchtime to clear up the stuff in the kitchen.
And it was on the table. And she just started
reading. And then she couldn't stop. And she read
it all. And she says to me that because she read
it she knows I kept caring about her all the time

when she was taking drugs. And then she starts crying again. And when she's crying she says she never stopped caring about me either even though it looked as though she did. And then she was just shaking her head and crying. And she said she never knew before how happy I was to get back from the home they put me in.

And we tried to have a normal night. Mum made us ravioli and salad and I put on the telly. And we watched it. Then she said I've got to go to bed otherwise I'm going to be too knackered to do anything properly at school and I need to because of the performance. And when she says that I ask if she's coming. And she says she hardly got anything done in the afternoon after coming home at lunchtime. And Mr Mieri wasn't happy about it at the shop. And there's still loads to do. But maybe they're going to finish tomorrow and if they do she'll come.

And I went to bed and she did too.

So I'm in bed now trying to write about what happened. And it feels better than last night felt. But all the time I've been thinking WHAT IF JON COMES BACK AND KICKS IN THE DOOR? Mum says he won't because she knows him. And if she's right then I'm glad about everything I did.

Thursday 26th of March

It's Thursday so now it's the last day before the performance. As soon as I got in the classroom Pete saw the plaster Mum put on my hand and he asked me about what happened. But I'm not telling him or it means I'll have to tell Liam about it and probably Marie too. Then next thing I'll probably get a CARE ORDER on me again.

So I just tell him I fell off my bike.

And Pete doesn't say any more about it.

And Nazrul's still away. And Pete said that means he's not in the performance now.

Then at breakfast he starts asking who's got someone coming to watch the performance. And it sounds like nearly everyone's got someone coming. Like Nathan's mum's coming and Raymond's foster mum and Raju's sister and Micah's nan. And I say my mum might be coming.

And no one starts dissing her and saying the
normal stuff they say about her because Pete's
there. But Raju says how Nathan's mum looks so
young she looks like she should still be at school.
And Nathan says she isn't. Then Pete says Nathan's
lucky if his mum's young because HIS MUM'S 187
YEARS OLD. And that makes him start chuckling
at his own jokes as usual.

Then after breakfast we're meant to tell everyone
all about our FEELINGS. And it's the same as
always. And then we've got to go to the hall
because Richard and Aaron are in there today.
And when we're lining up I hear Barry's saying,
"I'm going to watch myself if Mrs Doolally shows
up because she only escaped from THE FUNNY
FARM last week."
And Barry knows I heard. So he's looking as happy
as A PIG IN A DUSTBIN. But I just say, "You don't

know anything about what my mum's like."

And Pete didn't hear anyway. But he knows something's going on because he tells us he wants COMPLETE SILENCE.

Then it's the DRESS REHEARSAL and I don't know why it's called that but it is. And Richard and Aaron are teaching us together this time. And there's this microphone set up and all the chairs ready for the performance. And when we go in Micah goes to the microphone and thinks he can do some KILLER RAPPING into it. But it wasn't switched on so he just looked A BIT OF A PRAT. And that made Aaron get in a strop about anyone touching the microphone. And he said even if we're using the microphone to read out our poem we can't touch it.

And after that him and Richard were in a strop nearly the whole morning. And Pete wasn't in much of a good mood either because he kept

stopping everything and saying we had to TRY
HARDER and WAKE UP and STOP AMBLING
ABOUT LIKE CATS ON A HOT AFTERNOON.

And we had to practise everything like reading
out the poems. And the song with me doing the
xylophone. And all the different bits of drumming.
And also a PROCESSION IN which meant we were
going to come in for the performance doing the
STAMPING AND FINGER CLICKING we did with
Richard on Monday.
And they got us to do everything till we got it
right. But even so we didn't always get it right.
Paolo still forgot how his firebird feather poem
goes even though everyone else knows it all by
heart by now. And then he almost got in a fight
with Nathan because Nathan was dissing him for
not knowing it. But Nathan said it was just
PLAY FIGHTING and so did Paolo. So Pete didn't

make a big thing about that.

Then we spent ages doing THE ANGRY MUSIC.
And after it Aaron said I had to read out my
faithful horse poem. And I said I wasn't doing it.
And Pete said YES I WAS. And he said Micah was
doing a horse poem too so we could go up to the
microphone both together. And I didn't want to.
But I went there.

And Micah tried to read out his but he kept
laughing instead of reading it. And the microphone
made his laughing loud. And Aaron said DON'T
SMILE OR LAUGH IN THE PERFORMANCE
because our poems are good and the audience
will just think they're silly if we were smiling or
laughing. And I did mine but I was nearly laughing
too. And I felt I looked a complete plonker. And
from how people were looking at me when I sat
down I DID LOOK A COMPLETE PLONKER.

And some bits of the performance were all right.
But the FAST DRUMMING MUSIC kept going
wrong because Barry couldn't remember where he
was meant to do his TAMBOURINE SOLO.
And Aaron said he wanted Raymond to do his
poem about GOING IN THE BOILING WATER
AND COMING OUT OF IT AFTER because
it's good. And he said for him to do it in a BIG
VOICE. Then Raymond shouted it so it sounded
like it broke the microphone. And everyone was
laughing about that.
Then last of all we had to practise bowing when
the audience was clapping. And we had to go in a
line and put our arms round each other's shoulders
and then bow. And most of what we did was
pretty crap SO I DON'T EVEN KNOW IF
ANYONE'S ACTUALLY GOING TO CLAP.

Then after we did everything Richard started

saying this speech that seemed as if it was going to
go on until it got dark. And he's telling us A LOT
OF THINGS WERE GOOD and how IT'LL BE EVEN
BETTER TOMORROW because we'll be nervous
and he reckons that means you do it better. Then
we get another speech from Aaron saying that
when you do a good performance it's better than
EATING YOUR FAVOURITE FOOD or something
like that. Then they both looked at Pete. And I'm
thinking HE'S NOT GOING TO MAKE A FRIGGING
SPEECH TOO IS HE?
But Pete says, "It's going to be FAB AND
GROOVY. And I'm hungry so let's have our dinner."
Which was more like what I wanted to hear.

Then in the afternoon it's just me here because
it's Thursday. And I've been writing this. And I
also had to see Liam. And he was asking about
HOW THINGS ARE AT HOME? And also WHAT

271

HAPPENED TO MY HAND? And I didn't tell
him. But even so he kept asking until I nearly
died out of boredom. And it was like being back
in THE HOME when the psychologists there kept
asking questions about things that are normally
private things. So you say any old crap. Then
they LEAN FORWARD and pretend they're
VERY INTERESTED in what you say even though
underneath you can see they're thinking there's
nothing they can do to help you. But Liam
finally changes the subject and he asks what I'm
doing in the performance. And I say about my
XYLOPHONE TUNE and also how I'm meant to
read my HORSE POEM.

Then Liam comes out with this stuff about how
if I do it well then no one can ever take that
away from me so I'll be proud about it for the rest
of my life.

And I'm trying not to yawn.

And he says he reckons I'm going to MAKE UP
FOR WHAT HAPPENED LAST YEAR by doing a
good performance because he's noticed how good
my SELF-CONTROL is this week.

And I'm thinking YEAH? PERHAPS YOU SHOULD
HAVE COME ROUND FOR A CUP OF TEA IN
OUR KITCHEN YESTERDAY MORNING.

But then he just tells me I can go back to the
classroom. And when I come in Pete says, "Did you
talk to Liam about the performance?"

And I nod. And he asks, "What did he say?"

And I say, "He thinks I'm going to do a good
performance."

Then Pete says, "Yeah?" And looks like he doesn't
agree.

So I say, "What's that look meant to mean?"

And he says, "Well knowing you you're going to
accidentally tie your shoelaces together. Then
when you get up to read your poem you'll fall

flat on your face and everyone will fall about laughing!"

And that's Pete being a FUNNY MAN like usual.

Then I came home. And when I was coming up the steps I was thinking Jon might be there. But he wasn't there. And Mum got back earlier. And she'd bought some new big plates. And I said to her, "Wasn't that expensive?"

But she said she was getting extra money because of the stock-taking and we needed new plates anyway. And she didn't say any more about it. She just cooked shepherd's pie which is the best thing she cooks.

Then when we're eating I ask if she's finished the stock-taking. And she looks at the new plates and says, "Don't you dare smash them." And I said I'm not going to. Then she says there's still loads to do and tomorrow's going to be busy. And both of us just carry on eating.

Then I say to her, "So you can't come tomorrow."

And she says, "Even if I could go Jason, I don't know if I COULD GO."

And I say, "What?"

And she looks at her food. But she wasn't eating it. She just kept looking at it.

So I say, "WHAT'S THAT MEAN MUM?"

Then she says to me, "It's the way they look at me if I go there."

And I say, "Who?"

Then she says, "Liam, Marie, Wendy. The other parents there. You can see they're looking at me like I'm not fit to even be a mum."

And I say, "It's not even to do with them. I WANT YOU TO COME."

Then she gives this little sniff as if she's almost crying and she says, "I KNOW! But I saw in your book what the boys in your class say about me and then what Liam asks about me."

And I say, "Then come to it and then they'll see how you're just a normal mum really!"

And Mum didn't say anything. She just looks away. Then she shook her head a bit and said, "It's not as easy as you think Jason."

And I didn't know what to say back about that. So I just finished my shepherd's pie. Then I did the washing up. And Mum said thank you for doing it. But she didn't say anything more about tomorrow. And we didn't even talk about Jon. And that's what happened.

Friday the 27th of March

The first thing when I woke up was I was thinking
IT'S THE PERFORMANCE. And my stomach was
turning over and over about it. And Mum had to
go early again like on the other days. And when
she went she said make sure I get the minibus
all right.
And I went down after a bit so I was waiting for
Keith when he got there. And it was warmer out
now but still not exactly sunny.

Then at breakfast everyone in the class was pretty
quiet. And that's probably because everyone was
getting nervous about the performance. And Pete
says to us he thinks there's 50 PEOPLE coming.
And a man's coming to take pictures for the paper
and also the Mayor's wife's coming and some other
BIGWIG I never heard of.

Then Pete says to us WHAT ARE WE ALL GOING
TO DO AT THE WEEKEND? And Barry tells him
he's going fishing. And he's looking like everyone's
supposed to think that's the coolest thing anyone's
ever done. But it isn't. It's just FISHING. And I say
to Pete, "I'm going to watch the football."
Then the others say some different things.
And then Pete says he's GOING TO IRELAND
because he's going to try to defend THE TITLE he
won last year.
And Raju says, "What TITLE?"
And Pete says maybe he never told us but last year
he won the ALL IRELAND FROG-SWALLOWING
CHAMPIONSHIP.
And Micah said it wasn't true. But Pete said it
was. And he said he was going to try to do better
than his record which was SWALLOWING 15
FROGS IN 65 SECONDS.
Then Barry said, "Do you have to talk about that

when we're having breakfast?" And Pete starts laughing and changes the subject.

Then we did FEELINGS and some people said they were feeling NERVOUS. But I said I was feeling ALL RIGHT.

Then next thing you can hear the sound of people out in the corridor because the performance is starting at ten o'clock. And Richard comes in and Aaron has gone up to the other class who are in the performance which is C Class.
And Richard says everything's set up in the hall and some people are already in there and we're going to go first and then it's going to be C Class. And he asks if everyone's ready. And some people say YEAH. But to be honest I'm hoping Raymond's going to suddenly go completely barmy or something and start smashing things so the whole

thing gets called off. And Richard's looking at me because I think he's remembering what happened last year. And he asks if I think I can do it. And I say, "I don't know because I'M SCARED STIFF."

And Richard says that's NORMAL to get BUTTERFLIES IN YOUR STOMACH. But I said to him it didn't feel like BUTTERFLIES in my stomach. It was more like FRIGGING KANGAROOS. Then he told us when we get in the hall MAKE SURE WE LOOK AT THE AUDIENCE because that makes it easier. And try to play with EXPRESSION. Then he said it's only a school performance but we've got to think like we're PROFESSIONAL MUSICIANS IN A CONCERT.

Then he looked round at us lot gawping back at him. And it looked like he was going to say ACTUALLY YOU LOT MIGHT AS WELL JUST FORGET EVERYTHING I JUST SAID.

But anyway then we go down the corridor and wait outside the hall with Pete and Shabana and Richard. And everyone's in there because you can hear the sound of them talking all at once. And Aaron comes and waits with us too. And Shabana has got to go and get Raymond's asthma inhaler. Then Wendy's starting making some speech. And after it Richard says for us to start the FOOT STAMPING AND FINGER CLICKING rhythm. And we do the procession in. And inside there's the other boys in our school sitting at the front with the teachers. And there's lots of people on the chairs behind them. And they've all got this programme that Pete made which has got our names on it and the name of the performance which is THE FIREBIRD.

And the photographer man's standing by the windows with his camera. And there's Micah's Nan. And Barry's Mum who looks like about three

people tied together. And then Marie. But Mum's
not there.

Then we get to our places at the front. And
the first thing is Paolo and Nathan read their
FIREBIRD FEATHER POEMS. And Nathan does
it properly without smiling or anything. Then Paolo
does it too and he remembers it all which was a
bit of a miracle because I think it was the first
time he ever managed that.

Then it was the TRAVELLING TRAVELLING
TRAVELLING song. So I had to do the xylophone.
And just when I was getting the sticks I saw the
door of the hall open and it was Mum coming in.

And she looked embarrassed. And she couldn't see
a seat to sit on. But she found one near the back.
And she sat down. And then she looked at me and
what I was doing. And Aaron said that thing to us

282

about not smiling or laughing in the performance.
But I smiled because she was smiling at me. And I
think what I played on the xylophone was all right
from what you could tell from looking at Richard
and also from looking at Mum.

Then Raymond read out his poem about going in
the boiling water and coming out after. And the
camera man took about twenty pictures of him.
And a lot of people clapped really loudly when he
finished.

Then it's the angry poem with the angry music.
And I had to swap places for that. And so did
Barry Holmes. And it was when he nearly messed
up everything by being a COMPLETE PLANK AS
USUAL. Because he didn't look on the chair he
had to sit on. And there was a big shaker thing
there that he was meant to pick up and play.

But DUMBO BARRY sat down without looking. Then there's this massive cracking sound because the shaker's been broken to bits by his big bum. And he just stays sitting as if no one's going to notice if he doesn't get up. And he's staring up at Richard LIKE A DOG WITHOUT A HOME. But Richard gets him to stand up. And when he does all these beads or something that were in the shaker go scattering off the chair and across the floor. And everyone's trying not to laugh at it. But if you look in the audience Liam for example is almost falling off his chair because it's so funny. And the beads still keep falling off Barry's trousers. And in the end nobody's even trying to stop laughing any more and even Barry starts laughing at it. And Richard gets another shaker to give him and this time he manages not to sit on it.

Then we can do THE ANGRY POEM. And after it

I don't know what's next but from the way Aaron's staring at me and Micah like we're his best friends it looks like it's time for us to do the FAITHFUL HORSE POEMS.

And the hall's all quiet. And Micah gets up with the paper with his poem on it and he's going to the microphone.

But I stay sitting down BECAUSE I'M NOT DOING IT.

And Aaron sort of nods at me. But I look back and shake my head.

Then Pete gets up and says quietly, "Go on Jason. You can do it!"

And I say back quietly, "I CAN'T."

And Aaron looks like he's trying to make me get up by some sort of hypnotizing.

But I shake my head another time because what's going to make me stand up isn't what Pete's saying or how Aaron's looking at me. IT'S MY LEGS and they're not working because I NEVER STOOD UP AND READ OUT A POEM LIKE THAT BEFORE. And I DIDN'T WANT TO DO IT.

And Micah's standing waiting.

And I can feel like every eye in the whole place looking at me.

And Pete tries one more time and says, "COME ON!"

And I look down. And then everyone's probably thinking, "He's not doing it."

But I wasn't looking down because I wasn't going to do it. I was looking down to see if my shoelaces were tied together.

And they weren't. So I did it. I stood up and went there with Micah.

And first he read out what he wrote about his

faithful horse. And then I did my poem which
is this,

MY HORSE

My horse is blazing bright like gold and yellow.
My horse has got silvery eyes and my horse is strong.

He runs through burning flames or ice.
He runs so fast he swims in the wind.

And he can hide in walls.
And when I'm in trouble my faithful horse helps me.

And after it everyone's clapping like they liked
it. Mum, Liam, Wendy, Barry's Mum, Micah's Nan.
They're smiling because they listened to my horse
poem and they liked it. And then I sat down next
to Pete and said, "I'm going to GET YOU

for making me do that."

Then we did the last thing which was the FAST
DRUMMING. And up until then I didn't really care
if the performance was good or not. But when
we were doing the fast drumming the audience
started clapping with the rhythm we were doing.
And Raymond was WHACKING the djembe. And
I had the cowbell. And Barry managed to get his
solo on the tambourine in the right place. And
after his solo people started clapping him even
though the song wasn't even finished. And it wasn't
just his mum clapping either. Then Richard made
us go really loud. And the people who were there
were looking so pleased that I started feeling
pretty pleased too.

And then the bit my class was doing was over
and people were clapping us. And some of the
people stood up to clap. And so we did our bowing

in a line. But somehow the order of people got muddled because I found I was in the line standing next to frigging Barry Holmes. So I was meant to put my arm round him. And he was meant to put his arm round me. And someone was whistling. And Mum was looking like she was happy she came. And everyone was clapping on. So I did it. And the photographer man takes another picture. And I thought having to read out my frigging horse poem was bad enough. But having to stand like that with Barry Holmes was 50 times worse. And there's probably even going to be a frigging picture of it in the paper too.

Then C Class did their performance. And we sat at the side to watch it. Then there was more clapping. And we could stay for a bit so we could talk to the people who were there. And I go to where Mum is. And Liam goes there too. And he's saying thank you for her coming and saying she's looking well.

And she says to him, "Thanks. I AM well."

And I don't say much. But that's all right because Mum knows I'm happy she came.

And Pete stayed talking to people. So Shabana took us back to the classroom. And she said we were great. And Richard and Aaron showed up to say goodbye. And they said we were great. Then Wendy and Liam come and they said we were great. And then Pete came back and he said we were A LOAD OF RUBBISH and the reason he didn't come straightaway was because he had to get an ASPIRIN FROM THE FIRST AID BOX because he had such a headache. Which was him joking away because he's a funny man. OR AT LEAST HE THINKS HE IS.

Monday 30th March

There's only three pages left now. So I'm going
to write about today and then that'll mean I've
written in the whole of this journal book.
The weekend was all right because I watched
the football and also I went to the ramp. And
Ollie was there but not his mum. So there was no
ORGANIC APPLE JUICE but it meant we could
have a MASSIVE PILE UP without her getting
stressed out because she thought Ollie was going
to be dead at the bottom of it.
And Jon didn't show up like the last few weekends.
So I didn't have to wake up and find him on the
sofa. And Mum says he's not coming back now.
And you could see from her face she thinks that.
And maybe she's right and maybe she's not.
I don't know.

Then this week Richard and Aaron aren't at Heronford any more. So it's back to usual. Except one thing's different because I decided when I finish all this journal then I'm going to show it to Pete. And he can read it if he wants.

And I said that to Mum when she was ironing my school clothes yesterday. And she said DON'T SHOW IT because she says there's stuff in here that'll get her in trouble and everyone's going to know WHAT A TERRIBLE MUM SHE IS.

And I said to her, "Yeah. That's true. And it's why they let me come back from that home isn't it? Because they found out WHAT A TERRIBLE MUM YOU ARE."

And she smiled a bit then.

And I said to her, "They let me come back because it means you're a GOOD MUM."

And she said she's trying. And she carried on doing

the ironing. Then she said it's my book SO I CAN CHOOSE WHAT TO DO WITH IT.

And I told Pete just now he can read it when I finish this page. And he said, "Thanks Jason." And he said, "That's great," like he was surprised and also pleased.

And then he said to me, "How does it make you FEEL if someone else is going to read what you've written?" And I said to him, "ALL RIGHT."

AUTHOR'S NOTE

I taught in a school for boys with emotional and behavioural difficulties every year for over ten years. I was there as a visiting writer. This book is based on memories of those years. But the characters, the things that happen and the places where they happen are all imagined.

I wrote '*A Waste of Good Paper*' in Brazil. . . a long way from the world it describes. But I was lucky enough to have some books to hand which helped take me back to what I was writing about: *Jackie's Story* (the anonymous autobiography by a girl from East London published by Centerprise in 1984), *The Story of Tracy Beaker* by Jacqueline Wilson, *Shattered Lives* by Camila Batmanghelidjh and *Among the Thugs* by Bill Buford. In their different ways these special books helped me write this one, and I'd like to thank the authors for their work.

I'm grateful also to several storytellers who have passed down the Firebird story and brought it to life in my imagination, particularly Arthur Ransome and Michael Meade.

Thanks also to Adriana Meirelles, Rob Porteous, Steve Tasane, James and Celia Catchpole and Janetta Otter-Barry, who read what I was writing at different stages and helped sharpen it up.

And finally, I raise my hat to the many big-hearted teachers I've met working with young people with emotional and behavioural difficulties, and to those young people themselves who, against the odds, stood up and read out their poems.

Sean Taylor

Sean Taylor is an award-winning author of books for young readers of many different ages. His books include the *Purple Class* series of comic adventures set in an urban primary school, a collection of folktales from the Amazon called *The Great Snake*, and picture books for younger readers such as *Crocodiles are the Best Animals of All!*, *The Grizzly Bear With The Frizzly Hair* and *Who Ate Auntie Iris?*. Over the years he and his family have spent spells living in England (where he was born) and Brazil (where his wife is from).

www.blog.seantaylorstories.com